Potpourri of Praise

Heartwarming Stories of Faith from Around the World

WINEPRESS PUBLISHING
MUKILTEO, WA 98275

The Sweet Fragrance of Faith

Potpourri comes from two French words that describe the ancient practice of collecting flowers, herbs, and spices in a vessel for use as a room freshener. As the specially prepared mixture began to ferment, it gave off a delightful, exquisite fragrance.

The Apostle Paul spoke of sacrificial faith of believers as being "a sweet-smelling aroma, an acceptable sacrifice, well pleasing to God" (Philippians 4:18). When we meet with men and women whose faith has cost them something, or when we hear their stories, our lives are filled with this same fragrance Paul described; their stories become encouragements and incentives for our faith as well.

In our sheltered world of North America, we often expect Christianity to show up in life-styles we understand. In so doing, we miss the fragrant incense arising from faith being lived out in other parts of the world. In Eastern Europe, the South Seas, Africa, the Middle East, Asia, and India, faith in Christ and expressions of new life in Christ are just as real and often more heartwarming to observe than the kind we see here at home.

This is a book to display what faith in action looks like as the message of Jesus Christ penetrates and transcends cultural and political restraints. It is a *potpourri* of fragrant faith, collected from all over—stories to make you feel at home and at heart with fellow believers around the world.

Though very few missionaries are mentioned, these short biographical sketches are the evidence of God's blessing on their perseverance. The people featured in these stories are tributes to them; they are the "jewels" who will make up the "crowns" to be presented to these faithful workers when the enthroned Christ pronounces, "Well done, good and faithful servants" to them.

Some of the stories come from mission societies shown at the end of each article. All have been rewritten in third person to fit the flavor of this book.

Other articles are written in first person, about people we the authors have met. The initials at the end of each story (S.T.O. or W.W.) indicate who wrote or rewrote it.

Each story, we believe, should evoke from us prayers of thanksgiving to a gracious God, who responds to the prayer of faith from whatever dark corner of the world it arises.

Susan Titus Osborn
Wightman Weese

Contents

One

Pastor Ananda
A Burden for His Flock

India

He is no fool who gives what he cannot keep to gain what he cannot lose. — James Elliot

---

"Come visit my church," the quiet, little minister invited, looking at me with enormous compelling brown eyes. Rev. Ananda Maharajan was a student in my creative writing class at the India Communications Institute sponsored by Spiritual Overseers Service. He pastors a church in Dharavi, the largest slum in the world—an enclave of one million people located in Bombay, India. This dedicated Christian was born a Muslim, but he was orphaned at an early age. Raised in an Amy Carmichael Orphanage in India, he came to know Christ and dedicated his life to serving Him.

Ananda makes his home on a church compound in downtown Bombay because there is no housing available near the church he pastors. He rides his motorscooter to work every day. On Sundays, he preaches at the Good Shepherd Church at 11 a.m. At three auxiliary locations within the Dharavi area at 2, 4, and 7 p.m., he holds services for those who do not live within walking distance of the Good Shepherd Church.

On the afternoon I accepted the pastor's invitation, my driver diligently searched for the church. For almost an hour we drove along the narrow streets of Dharavi, congested with vendors hawking their wares. Children and adults usurped the right-of-way, walking slowly in front of our vehicle. Time seemed to drag on this humid, August afternoon.

1

Eventually we found the Good Shepherd Church. Ananda smiled warmly as he greeted us with a friendly handshake. He led us inside, his white Anglican robes flowing behind him and adding an air of distinction to this humble man of God.

Long fluorescent lights and spinning fans hung from the ceiling. In the center of the hand-carved black teak altar stood a lattice-work cross flanked by ornate brass candlestick holders. Two bouquets of roses, daisies, and orchids also graced the altar table. Sun filtered through the turquoise-painted window bars, forming geometric designs on the peeling blue walls. The church had almost no furniture.

"We left only one pew which we use for communion, so it takes a long time to serve over one thousand people each Sunday," Pastor Ananda explained, "but without pews, we have more room for the congregation." He ran his fingers through his gray hair which was receding at the temples. The burden of pastoring fifteen hundred slum-dwelling families caused Ananda to look older than his forty-two years.

I stared at the off-white tiled floor of this small, unpretentious church and tried to imagine how one thousand parishioners could possibly sit on that floor during an entire church service.

Ananda spoke of plans to expand the walls of this hundred-year-old church. "When the construction is completed, more people can be seated. Also a house is being built behind the church. When it is finished, I can live closer to the families of my congregation."

Hammers pounded in the background—evidence that work was underway. Sari-clad women carried large platters of earth on their heads, removing it from the construction area. As they passed the doorway, bracelets jingled on their arms.

The message preached that morning in Tamil, the dialect spoken by the congregation, was based on Matthew 11:28-30. "Come to Me, all you who labor and are heavy laden, and I will give you rest. Take My yoke upon you and learn from Me, for I am gentle and lowly in heart, and you will find rest for your souls. For My yoke is easy and My burden is light."

Pastor Ananda told his flock that Jesus welcomes people who are weighted down beneath their burdens. The majority of Ananda's congregation are tanners and leather toolers. They are shunned by local Hindus who consider it a sin to kill cows or to use their skins. This chosen occupation will continue to keep these individuals in Dharavi, held prisoner by the only trade they know.

When we left the Good Shepherd Church that afternoon, hundreds of children stood outside. On the way to the car I shook hands with all I could touch. As the driver pulled slowly away, more children reached their hands inside the car to shake hands with the blonde American who had come to visit their pastor. I turned around for one last look and saw them waving goodbye.

As we drove through the rows of shanties made of slabs of wood, rusty corrugated iron, and plastic sheeting, I marveled that we had found the small church in this sea of humanity. An ox pulling a cart filled with blocks of ice, lumbering along the street behind us, reminded me again of Pastor Ananda's message.

Jesus encourages Pastor Ananda and the slum-dwellers of Dharavi. He also encourages us to take His yoke upon our shoulders. When He said that His yoke is easy He meant well-fitting. In Old Testament times the ox was brought to the carpenter shop and measured. The yoke was roughed out of wood, and then the ox was brought back to try it on. The carpenter carefully adjusted the yoke so it would fit well and not chafe the ox's neck. Each yoke was custom-made to fit each ox.

Pastor Ananda's burden for his flock, however heavy, is carried with joy and compassion. It fits him well. Each of us has our own divinely designed yoke—our own job to do. Suddenly I felt a renewed strength to wear the yoke God has fashioned for me.

Looking Inward: Sometimes my burdens seem overwhelming, and I cry out, "Lord, I can't cope with all this. I cannot function under these circumstances." Yet, He challenges me to learn from Him, to rest in Him. He will never place a yoke upon us that is more than we can bear.

Looking Outward: God has given a special job to each of us. He expects us to use the talents and tools He has given us to accomplish the task at hand. One person may go to the mission field in Bombay, another may provide financial support. Someone else may cook meals for a shut-in neighbor. Another individual's past, difficult experiences may give her empathy so she can furnish emotional understanding and encouragement to a friend. Remember our yokes are easy. They fit well.

S.T.O.
Spiritual Overseers Service (SOS)

Two

Asanka
The Twelfth Time

Sri Lanka

As I look back over my footprints, I am grateful for the stamina of God. — Tim Hansel, *When I Relax I Feel Guilty*

Asanka stretched out on the cot at Power House in Colombo, Sri Lanka. One remaining button held his shirt together over his thin chest. His body appeared to be wasting away. He looked at me with eyes that were sunken and hollow. As we became acquainted, I asked him what had happened to his left arm. He explained that when he was inoculated against polio as a child, his arm shriveled.

Rolling to a more comfortable position, he spoke sadly of his past. "I married a Christian girl at a young age, and soon we had two boys to provide for. I had promised Kalyani she could go to church after we were married, but I later changed my mind. You see I come from a Buddhist background."

Asanka told me how tension in the young family had grown as the responsibilities increased. Asanka forbad his wife to go to church, while he turned to heroin as a solace. Soon Asanka became addicted, and he was no longer able to provide for his family.

Kalyani realized that she must earn a living. Since no jobs were available in her small Sri Lankan village, she went to Saudi Arabia where she found work as a housemaid. In her absence, her parents took care of the young boys, ages two and five.

Asanka continued his story. "Every week, Kalyani faithfully sent her paycheck to me." He paused, and tears filled his eyes as he recalled the painful events. Softly he confessed, "I spent her entire year's wages on drugs. I've tried time and time again to stop, but I can't do it by myself."

Asanka had hospitalized himself eleven times, taking a methadone treatment. Each time he failed. He desired to conquer the drug habit; he longed to be with his wife and children. However, heroin had become his family and his god.

One of his best friends had been Ransinghe, the unchallenged leader of the gang in Asanka's small village. Ransinghe, a tall young man in his early twenties, stole from the elderly as well as the local merchants—anything to support his heroin drug habit of many years. Then one day, he disappeared.

Nine months later, Ransinghe returned to the village a changed man. He helped one widow patch her leaking roof in time for monsoon season. Fruit had been the easiest item to steal in the past. Now, instead of stealing it, he assisted the fruit merchant in repairing the rotten timbers on his porch.

At the time, Asanka wondered what had changed this former gang leader. Finally he gathered enough courage to ask, "Ransinghe, what has happened to you, man? Why did you disappear?"

Ransinghe replied, "I went to Power House, friend. It changed my life." Power House is a rehabilitation program, a Christian Community Concern project sponsored by Shepherd's Heart Ministries for drug abusers located near Colombo. "Why don't you try it, too?" he asked.

Asanka was afraid to go to Power House, afraid to fail again. But Asanka weighed his options and came up empty-handed, so he finally decided to follow his friend's advice. Still in the back of his mind he wondered, *What will happen this time?*

Now turning his thoughts to the present, Asanka once again repositioned his slight frame on the cot at Power House and said, "Only Jesus can cure me. Only Jesus can take away the pain, the craving."

When Asanka first arrived at Power House and entered the rehabilitation program, the other fourteen recovering addicts took turns staying with him twenty-four hours a day. They were able to help him emotionally because they had all been through the pain of withdrawal themselves.

Raising up on one elbow, Asanka continued, "The other brothers prayed with me. They never left me when I needed them."

I nodded in understanding. Asanka struggled for the right words to express his feelings.

A glimmer of hope lit his tired-looking eyes. "I wrote my wife in Saudi Arabia yesterday. I told her that I, too, am now a Christian. I said that I grow stronger every day. I clear the land and cultivate the fields with the other brothers. We sell the coconuts to help pay our way."

Since Asanka found Jesus, he has discovered his own self-worth. He is learning to be productive, to take responsibility for himself. He failed eleven times to conquer the drug habit by himself. Perhaps the twelfth time will be different, and he can soon be reunited with his young family.

One of the other brothers came into the room. He sliced a deep-red pomegranate and shared it with us. I picked through the multitude of seeds to eat the delicious pulp. Then I glanced out the window at the twenty-foot pomegranate tree. Many years ago someone had planted a seed where a fruit-bearing tree now stood. The slender branches hung low, weighted down by a bounty of fruit.

Only God knows how many trees can grow from a fist full of pomegranate seeds, I thought.

My eyes turned again to Asanka. Ransinghe had planted a seed. It was growing through Asanka's changed life. Perhaps when he is able to return to his village, his friends and family members will notice the transformation and will ask, "What has happened to you, man?"

Asanka will have a wonderful opportunity to tell the people of his predominantly Buddhist village about the miracle Jesus Christ has worked in his life.

Just as Asanka watched Ransinghe's actions, often non-Christians carefully observe the way we live our lives. They aren't affected so much by what we say as by what we do. If we are to plant seeds by proclaiming the gospel, our words need to be backed up every day by the way our faith is demonstrated in our lives.

Looking Inward: I am incapable of conquering in my own strength the problems that arise in my life. Sometimes I become discouraged when I can't reason out a solution in my mind. But when I turn the situation over to the Lord and allow Him to solve the problem, I immediately feel a sense of relief. Often He shows me a workable solution that I never would have imagined.

Looking Outward: Once when I was going through a particularly difficult time in my life, an acquaintance remarked, "You are always talking about God. Now that the going is tough, let's see if you live what you say." This incident made me realize how important my actions are and what an effect they can have on others.

S.T.O.
Christian Community Concern
Shepherd's Heart Ministries

Three

My Friend Augustin

Romania

God and I have this in common—we both love His Son, Jesus Christ. —Lance Zavitz

---

At the time, the Iron Curtain was still iron—rusty, but strong, cold, and forbidding. It was Saturday afternoon in Burcharest, Romania, during the darkest days of the Nicolae Ceausescu regime. Knowing I was probably being followed by the secret police, I took a circuitous route to find the Baptist Church on a street called Michail Bravu.

The front door was locked, but I could hear what sounded like workmen inside. Circling the building, I finally found a side door open and stepped inside. Three men were toiling away, one about twenty years old and another who could have been his father. The third was a very old gentleman with a thick white moustache. He wore workman's coveralls, and an artisan's brimless cap was pulled down severely over his forehead.

The minute I stepped inside, the sawing and hammering and the loud talking and laughing stopped. They stood like statues. I could almost feel their cold stares during the awkward silence.

"English?" I asked.

No response.

Then, I tried my French: "Anglais?"

The youngest spoke first. "Yes," he said. "I . . . English, a little."

I saw I wasn't going to get far with them. Their quizzical looks continued. Living under heavy surveillance for years had made

8

them, like everyone I had met since I arrived, suspicious and reluctant to talk to anyone they didn't know, especially a foreigner.

I had come to Romania to do research for a book, to learn more about a man named Joseph Tson, who had been exiled for more than ten years in America. Years before, Joseph had often preached in this same church.

In spite of the coolness of their reception, something inside told me that these three were believers, here volunteering their Saturday to do church repairs. I sensed it was safe to tell them why I had come. Perhaps then they would talk to me.

"I have come from America. . . from Joseph," I said, and pointed toward the pulpit.

That did it! Their eyes and mouths sprang open. Almost in unison, they repeated. "Joseph! Joseph! America!"

I wasn't prepared for what happened next. The old man rushed over and wrapped me in a vise-like embrace. Then he pointed to himself and pronounced his name, over and over, "Augustin, Augustin." He thought it should mean something to me. Or perhaps he wanted me to tell Joseph I had met "Augustin."

The circle closed quickly. I was instantly a part of the body. They offered me tea from a battered tea kettle kept warm on a small gas burner in a back room. They wanted to show me the new sections of the church. One pointed to my camera. The English speaker asked me to make some photographs to show Joseph, who hadn't seen the church since they had remodeled it. Then they asked me to stand in the pulpit, where Joseph had stood, while one of them borrowed my camera and took a photo of me standing beside Augustin.

Five minutes ago I was a stranger, arousing only suspicion. Now I was a cherished friend, feeling all the love Christian brothers could show me, despite the language barrier.

None of them had seen Joseph for more than ten years. But every Sunday afternoon his voice came back to them in an hour-long gospel broadcast, produced in America and beamed by Christian radio into Romania. Somehow just my being there with them gave them a tangible connection with their beloved friend.

How like God's family! How like God's love! Once again I remembered the Lord's own words to His disciples. "I do not say to you that I shall pray to the Father for you; for the Father Himself loves you, because you have loved Me" (John 16:26-27).

These men, with their smiles, their handshakes and embraces, showered me with affection — not because of who I was, but because of their love for a man they hadn't seen for more than ten years. It was as if they were saying, "If you are Joseph's friend, then we love you, too."

I stayed with them as long as I dared. Fearing that someone might have followed me there, I reluctantly said goodbye and left.

"To leave" is a strange expression, which can mean "go away" or "leave behind." I felt I was leaving part of myself with them and taking part of them with me. And in a different way, I was leaving people I loved — not because of who they were but because we loved and served the same Person. In the realm of spirit-to-spirit communication that goes beyond words, we all felt the powerful love of the Father — because we both loved His Son. Language, customs — not even Iron Curtains get in the way of that kind of bond.

I had come, feeling I was a stranger. I left, sensing I was a beloved brother.

Looking Inward: Even in a crowd, I sometimes feel alone, forgotten, or neglected. I easily forget that wherever I go the family of God surrounds me. The Church, made up of people like me, are specially prepared agents of God who will make me feel a part of the family, if only I'll crack open the door of my life and let them in.

Looking Outward: Somewhere — out there, somewhere — today, someone has lost sight of the magnitude of the great family of believers. What is a person going to see in my life today that will remind him of Christ. How can I make him feel "safe at home" in my presence?

W.W.
Romanian Missionary Society (RMS)

Four

Caught In
Colombia's Crossfire

Columbia

All of our theology must eventually become biography. —
Tim Hansel

Carlos walked slowly up the path toward the little church in Colombia, near the Venezuelan border. His Bible tucked securely under his arm, he hummed to himself, recounting his day-long, peaceful fishing trip. But after long hours on the river, his tired body and slight limp reminded him that old age was creeping up.

Stooping a little, he entered the dim church, a fellowship started through the efforts of the Evangelical Alliance Mission (TEAM). One lone gasoline lamp cast eerie shadows on the walls. Taking off his hat, Carlos slid to his usual place on the third bench from the back. As his eyes adjusted, he recognized familiar faces.

He joined in the singing, sending praises to God through the open door and out into the night. After a short time, Pastor Martinez stepped to the pulpit and began the sermon.

Deep in concentration on Pastor Martinez's sermon, Carlos barely noticed the strangers who slipped through the door.

Suddenly, one of the men in the back nodded toward the door. Several more intruders entered the church and took strategic places in the room. On cue, they pulled out guns and pointed them at the members of the congregation.

The leader of the guerrilla band strutted down the center aisle to the front and dragged the astounded pastor out a side door. Everyone watched in shocked silence. Fear hung in the air.

11

The leader returned, apparently leaving another in charge of the captured pastor. He stepped into the pulpit and addressed the congregation. His words cut the silence. "Those of you who believe this God stuff come forward."

For a moment, no one stirred. Then, pulled by some inner strength, Carlos stood and walked up the center aisle to the front. In a quiet voice he said, "I love Jesus."

Two guerrillas grabbed his arms and brusquely herded him outside.

Then one by one, others stood and walked to the front. They, too, were escorted outside to join Carlos and Pastor Martinez. At last, only a few were left sitting in the pews. The guerrilla leader stared at each individual, but no one else came forward. He addressed the remaining group. With a look of disdain and contempt he shouted, "Out! Out! All of you! You have no right to be here. Only those with courage to stand up for what they believe can stay."

At a signal from the leader, several guerrillas herded the remaining people out the front door of the church. They walked away without turning back.

Then the guerrillas escorted the amazed, faithful Christians back into the church and seated them in the pews. The pastor was returned to his pulpit and ordered to continue preaching.

This time, the story ended on a positive note. But many other situations like this have ended in violence. According to the press, Latin America, where 35 percent of all the terrorist acts in 1988 took place, is more affected by such warring factions than any other place in the world.

The Church in Columbia has not been exempt from bloodshed either. There, executions based solely on one's faith are not as common as in other places. Yet, in other areas where guerrillas have taken over, a number of believers have been killed. Because of their Christian convictions, they feel they can't support these leaders, financially or philosophically. They refuse to pay guerrilla-imposed quotas, and they refuse to cooperate with government agents or to attend "indoctrination" meetings.

For months, Manuel Sumalabek, a prosperous farmer and active member of TEAM's largest church in Colombia, ignored threats on his life. When he refused to bend to extortion he was brutally murdered. But feeding the guerrilla groups, who pass through, is equally dangerous because of right-wing hit teams. Rural people who are suspected of cooperating with guerrillas are executed without trial.

Drug traffickers pressure Christians farmers, many barely subsisting on corn sales, by offering them millions of pesos to raise marijuana or to process cocaine for them. Or they may approach evangelical students and tempt them with enough money to attend college if they agree to transport packages of cocaine as they travel abroad to study. Or a widow might be offered an exorbitant amount of money for a store that is losing money. To drug dealers, this area is worth a fortune because of its location.

Many of these Colombian Christians have known the struggle of choosing to do right, knowing they may go hungry as a result. Yet the inner joy and peace, and their confidence in God's supply, can only be explained by the kind of faith Paul urged upon Timothy: "You therefore must endure hardship as a good soldier of Jesus Christ. No one engaged in warfare entangles himself with the affairs of this life, that he may please him who enlisted him as a soldier" (2 Timothy 2:3,4).

In the midst of such dangers, many people of those lands in Central and South America are reexamining their spiritual resources. They realize that faith in the state church, in spiritism, or in materialism cannot help them. Christians in Colombia, like Carlos, know what it means to trust God in times of danger and trial. Because of their belief in God and their courageous response, they have a unique opportunity to share their faith.

Looking Inward: Our theology must be lived out in our lives to have any effect on those around us. We must know what we believe and why. If we are truly committed to Christ, we are willing to lay our lives on the line — willing to die for Him.

Looking Outward: God's people around the world must pray for God's miraculous intervention in these difficult situations believers face in such troubled lands. God expects His people to take prayer seriously at all times—not just during crisis situations. Our responsibility is to pray faithfully, for the people in countries like Colombia, who are now struggling against the forces of darkness.

S.T.O.
Evangelical Alliance Mission (TEAM)

Five

Don Chema
Loved the Darkness

Guatemala

Mere change is not growth. Growth is the synthesis of change and continuity, and where there is no continuity there is no growth. —C.S. Lewis, *Selected Essays*

Don Chema loved the darkness. In his small village he worked in the coffee fields by day. But when night came, he would slip away to his other life, involved in witchcraft, putting curses on people and trying to communicate with the dead.

At home Don Chema was impossible to live with. His wife Marcela was often yanked around by her pigtail, and if Don Chema's food was not ready when he wanted it, he would slap her viciously, or drag her around, yelling curses at her.

Don Chema still loved the night. But something happened to him. One day he came in contact with some missionaries from CAM International and heard about the gospel. Although he couldn't read, he began to listen quietly to the message being preached each Sunday as he gathered with the believers in his village to hear the Bible being taught.

Before, Don Chema slipped out into the night to work his evil spells. But something changed in him to make his nightly mission take on a different light. It was Marcela who became the object of his concern. Instead of seeking out power and calling up curses, he was now praying to the God he had come to know. Instead he was now calling down blessings on Marcela, praying that she would believe the gospel and become a believer like him.

After so many years of his bad behavior, Marcela remained skeptical. But little by little she saw the change taking place in her husband. Before he would yell and strike her. Now when he returned from the coffee fields, he would sit patiently on a large rock outside their little home, waiting for the meal to be prepared. Before when Marcela would scold him, he would yell and strike her. Now he quietly walked outside and sat on his rock.

"What is the matter with you?" Marcela asked. "What has come over you? Are you sick?"

It was the question Don Chema had been waiting to hear. He began to explain to her the message he had been hearing from the Bible, that he believed it and accepted it, and that it was God who had changed his life. Still Marcela was skeptical.

Unmoved, Don Chema kept up his nightly vigil, praying for Marcela to see the truth. Don Chema began to read the Bible he had been given. He tried to explain to Marcela that everyone was a sinner and needed to come to Christ. He told her that both Adam and Eve had sinned, but Marcela couldn't believe it.

One Sunday at church Don Chema brought his Bible to the missionary and said, "My wife said that if I can show her from the Bible that Eve was the first one to eat the forbidden fruit that she will accept this as fact. Then she would believe."

Don Chema had hoped that showing Marcela the passage would change her immediately. But too many years of living with him made her skeptical still.

Don Chema, accustomed to dark nights and evil works, continued his nightly prayer vigils. He would go often to the little chapel and sit for hours in the darkness praying. Then one day, what he had been praying for actually happened. Jesus had said, "But you, when you pray, go into your room, and when you have shut your door, pray to your Father who is in the secret place; and your Father who sees in secret will reward you openly" (Matthew 6:6). Don Chema's closet was the darkness of the chapel, but the answer he received openly came the day Marcela entered the chapel and prayed to receive Christ as her Savior.

Looking Inward: Sometimes we think God should change everything about us when we give ourselves to Him. Often many things about us do change. Other things about our personality God won't change, for He intends to use us as He made us. Don Chema's love of the darkness made the nightly prayer vigil a place of delight. Out of his own personal darkness came forth light that reached out and blessed his wife.

Looking Outward: When the light of God shines into our lives, we become light bearers to those who are still in darkness. The clearest light is God's Word. But the method God often uses is the light He has put within us. Others see the change in us and recognize it as the Light of Life.

W.W.
CAM International

Six

Col Taw Hal
Slow but Steady

Burma

Perseverance . . . keeps honor bright. —William Shakespeare

The powerful engine of the long-tailed boat sputtered momentarily, then roared into full-throttled life. British journalist Dan Wooding and Brother David, a former American marine then involved in taking Bibles into China, were beginning their short journey across the brown, fast-flowing Salween River. They traveled from Thailand into "Kawthoolei," a 30,000 square mile virgin mountain wilderness, a "liberated zone" of Burma, claimed by the unique Karen tribe.

Soon the pair sighted the trading gate of Wangkha, the headquarters of the Karen National Liberation Army's 101st Battalion (Special Forces). With the eager help of soldiers from one of the most extraordinary guerrilla groups in the world, Dan and David scrambled up the river bank.

They discovered that what makes this army so remarkable is they are unpaid. Many are Christians, and their leadership is almost entirely evangelical. Though in a nation dominated by Buddhism and animism, these fighting men in this Christian oasis carry Bibles in their pockets. They fast and pray whenever anticipating attacks by the enemy in this genocidal war.

"When I was shown a sign at a customs' post, I soon realized that the Karens are unique in this country that supplies much of the world's opium. The sign warned that anyone caught trafficking

17

in drugs `shall be punished severely or even suffer the death penalty,'" Wooding said.

The Karens' long-running fight began shortly after the British handed over Burma to the Burmese. The Karen people, originating in Mongolia, didn't want to be part of "the Burmese way to socialism." They desired to continue their unique and puritanical way of life unhindered.

The Karens were provoked to arms in January 1949 after two brutal massacres by the Burmese Army, including one in which Karen Christians were murdered during a Christmas Eve service. Since then, more than 10,000 of them have died in this war, one of forty wars presently raging in Burma.

These people were first evangelized by American missionary Adoniram Judson, who arrived in Burma in 1813. By 1934, he had translated the entire Bible as well as a number of tracts into the Karen language. Thousands turned to Christ and now, out of their three million population, it is estimated that seventy-five percent of the Karens are believers.

Wooding, the founder and international director of ASSIST (Aid to Special Saints in Strategic Times), soon discovered that many of the Karen military leaders model themselves after Old Testament leaders. Meeting in a secret camp, which has since been destroyed by an attack by Burmese forces, Colonel Taw Hal told Dan and Brother David, "Gideon was a good major, so I follow his ways."

Colonel Hal fingered his well-used Bible and went on, "I am a Christian, and I firmly believe God is still a miracle-working God. I believe He will perform another miracle with us."

With tears in his eyes he added, "I would ask Christians all over the world to pray that the Burmese would not have us as their enemies anymore. Pray that we could be friends again."

Rose Kho Thaw, a Baptist, told the visitors how much she appreciated Christian groups who brought them Bibles. "Do you know that the soldiers carry the pocket Bibles? They take them everywhere. Some carry the Bible as a talisman, but many are deep believers in it," she said. "If they find time to rest under the trees, they take out their Bibles and read them. They remember what they have been taught from childhood, and they get inspired that way. The Bible helps a lot."

When asked how Christians from the rest of the world could help the Karens, she replied, "By praying for us and coming to us." Tears filled her eyes as she continued, "We are really suffering for the Lord. Many of our people have been killed. We don't have a place anymore. We don't have land for our homes. Now we have refuge camps."

Burma's hard-line military dictatorship, which came to power in 1988 following a coup, has stepped up its campaign to defeat the Karens. Daily attacks on Karen positions are causing concern to the Karen leadership who would now like a "just and rational" settlement of their dispute, something the Burmese totally reject.

So will the Karens finally capitulate in their long fight against the Burmese?

"No way," say the Karens.

Some Burmese deride the Karens by calling them, "Slow."

But the Karens counter with the folklore tortoise motto: "Slow and steady wins the race."

The Apostle Paul wrote in Philippians 3:14, "I press toward the goal for the prize of the upward call of God in Jesus Christ." The Karens press toward the mark of victory — one that will allow them to practice their faith unhindered.

Looking Inward: Overanxious as we are, we demand that things happen on our timetable instead of God's. In this illustration, the Karens give us a wonderful example of perseverance. Inch by inch, we can press forward to win the race, too.

Looking Outward: Few of us are outwardly persecuted for our faith. Yet, little things crowd into our lives, causing us to lose sight of heavenly goals. We must keep our eyes focused on Jesus and press on, slow and steady, to claim the prize He has in store for us.

S.T.O.
Aid to Special Saints in Strategic Times (ASSIST)

Seven

Dawa's Story
Angelic Flames

Ecuador

The Christian character is the flower of which sacrifice is the seed. —Fr. Andrew SDC, *The Gift of Life*

More than thirty-five years have passed, but the story of the five young missionaries dying on the banks of the Curaray River in Ecuador lives on. All around the world as the story is told of what followed that dark day, January 8, 1956, of these men and their martyrdom, it continues to impact many lives. Over the years, hundreds of men and women have dedicated their lives to serve Christ on the basis of these missionaries' example.

Many of those who heard the story didn't hear of the effects these deaths had there in the jungles of Auca country. Not everyone knew that Gikita, the Auca who led the group on the killing spree that day, was the first to become a believer in that village. Later ninety-five percent of that village became believers. Nor, do many know that a few years later, one of the killers, Yowe, began praying about trying to reach another group of Auca's living nearby. Despite the danger that he would be speared, as he had taken part in spearing the strangers who brought the gospel into his territory, he wanted to reach out to them.

The Aucas, known to kill off whole families they didn't like, had reduced their numbers drastically. Sometimes entire small villages were speared to death by people of another village. Often one family would attack another. One family group of 200 in a matter of years had been reduced to about 40 as a result of these whimsical stabbings with palm lances. Fearful of all strangers, suspecting them of being cannibals, the Aucas looked with suspicion on anyone they didn't know. A new person arriving unannounced was likely to be killed immediately.

"You will be killed," his family protested, when Yowe announced his plans to go to a village down the river.

"Suppose I am," he replied. "If God tells me to go I must obey. And, if I am killed, God will send someone else to them as he sent others to us," he added, referring to the five martyrs and those who followed them to Auca country with the gospel.

Few also know that ten years later one of the Waodani Aucas was martyred by his own cousin, a man from a nearby group he was trying to reach with God's Word.

Sacrifice inspires sacrifice. It has always been that way, as Jesus said: "Freely you have received, freely give" (Matthew 10:8). "Still, it seemed like such a waste," some had said of the death of the five men. Over the years many have thought about that dark day, as they read the stories and look at the graphic photos taken by a *Life* magazine photographer and the film left in the cameras of the dead men. "Where was God when all of this was happening? Didn't He care? What a terrible way to die," many had said.

Rachel Saint's brother, Nate, was among the men slain. Not discouraged, Rachel continued working with an Auca woman, Dayuma. Rachel's efforts opened up Auca country to the gospel (Rachel has recently passed away).

Years later, an entirely different picture of what happened that day came to light during a visit to the site of the martyrdom. Olive Leifeld, who had been married to Pete Fleming, one of the martyred missionaries, returned with her second husband to visit the scene of her former husband's death thirty-five years before. Rachael Saint, who arranged for the visit, asked Kimo, one of the former killers, to act as their guide. Kimo, now a pastor, arrived with his wife, Dawa, and helped pole the canoe carrying the visitors to the fateful beach.

"Where was the tree house? Where was the fire the missionaries built?" Olive asked.

Kimo recounted the events as if they happened yesterday. In animated fashion, he began to act it out. "Right here where I am standing, we speared two of them in the back," he bluntly replied.

Rachel, concerned that the story was becoming too graphic for Olive, tried to change the subject. She turned to Kimo's wife and asked, "Where were you that day, Dawa?"

Dawa pointed to a high ridge behind the beach. "I was right there. By sunset we were all up there, and the bodies were still lying on the sand. Then suddenly a strange thing happened," she said, sweeping her hand broadly along the whole scene of the tragedy. "In the sky all along there—we saw a whole host of *cowode* (spirit beings), men and women dressed in beautiful clothes, singing what we now know to be God's songs, with musical instruments. And it was as if there were a hundred flashlights flashing. We were very afraid. We thought they were devils . . . then suddenly there were none."

Then Kimo turned to Olive's husband, Dr. Leifeld, and tried to explain their fearful reaction that evening. "You remember, doctoro, (doctor) when the disciples were riding in a dugout canoe (boat) and suddenly they saw "Itota," (the Lord) walking on the water and said, "It's a devil!" Way back then we knew nothing about God, and like the story in God's Carvings (the Bible,) we too were very much afraid."

Where was the Lord that dark day of January 8th, 1956, we ask? And why didn't He do something to avenge for his servants whose bodies lay there, strewn out on the beach and floating in the river?

Where was He? Dawa has given us the answer. He was just where we would expect Him to be — hovering there over that sad scene, with a host of angelic beings, directing a welcoming concert for their spirits rising to meet Him. Evidently, it was too important an event for the story to be swallowed up in the jungle darkness. It seems as if God had to mark the occasion, even if the angelic appearance was witnessed by only a handful of spirit-darkened jungle Indians.

Angelic flames of light and heavenly choirs, accompanied by celestial harps and trumpets, turned a scene of earthly tragedy into a scene of heavenly triumph. From what they saw that day, and from "God's Carvings" the Aucas learned what the Psalmist wrote: "Precious in the sight of the Lord is the death of His saints" (Psalm 116:15).

Looking Inward: A thousand of our deeds of kindness go unnoticed, and we are tempted to feel hurt and sorry for ourselves. Yet the only One in the universe whose view of us is of eternal importance sees every kind thought, every costly sacrifice, every drink of cool water given in His name.

Looking Outward: Malcolm Muggeridge, in his book, *Jesus: The Man Who Lives*, said "Ultimately on the cross Jesus gave all of his blood, to the very last drop, not to revive one patient for the remainder of a waning life, but to vivify all mankind forever." Every sacrifice offered in Jesus' name, whether we want to believe it boldly, is an eternal act that holds the possibility of universal consequences.

W.W.
Gospel Missionary Union (GMU)
Story adapted from "Operation Auca," from *The Gospel Message* (Vol. 99, #2), a publication of Gospel Missionary Union, used by permission.

Eight

The Dog Bite
And the Atheist

France

Suffering is a form of gratitude to experience, or an opportunity to experience evil and change it into good. —Saul Bellow, *Hertzog*

The two girls, Renate and Cindy, showed up at the meeting of Operation Mobilization team members, Cindy wearing a bandage on her wrist. Renate, the West German girl, turned to her American friend and said. "Cindy, you tell them what happened." She laughed. "After what happened, you deserve to tell it."

Cindy told of their visit in a quiet neighborhood of a French city. "We knocked at the door of a home, and a very severe looking woman appeared. When we told her why we were there. She explained quietly that she was a atheist. 'No thank you,' she said, quietly but coldly. 'I don't want your Bible calendars. My conscience is my Bible.' She then closed the door abruptly."

Disappointed, the two girls crossed the street to House Number 22. The house was fenced in, but the woman came to the gate and listened to the girls. Cindy was reaching through the bars of the gate to hand the woman a calendar. Suddenly, out of nowhere, a huge dog appeared. It snarled and jumped at the outstretched arm, biting down fiercely on Cindy's wrist, and refused to let go. The woman stood by quietly, as if she hadn't seen what happened. Wresting her arm free from the vicious grip, Cindy grasped her bleeding wrist, twisting in pain.

"No, thank you," the woman said. "I don't want any of your calendars." Turning around and walking back inside the house, the woman closed the door and left the startled girls standing there, wondering what to do about Cindy's painful, bleeding wrist.

"The atheist woman," one of them thought. Rushing back across the street, they knocked on the door again.

The woman returned, and seeing that Cindy was about to faint from the pain, ushered them quickly inside. She began to treat the torn wrist. The pain was so great that Cindy fainted. She woke to see the woman, looking tenderly at her, putting a dressing on the wrist.

"What cult do you belong to?" the woman asked.

"It isn't a cult," Cindy explained. The girls told of their mission, how they traveled through cities, sharing their Message about Jesus Christ and distributing literature.

The woman seemed genuinely moved at what the girls were doing. She listened, asked a number of questions, and turned the subject to such matters as history, philosophy, politics, and geography. Each time, Renate and Cindy turned the conversation back to God, what Christ had done, and how to find eternal life.

It was a different woman who saw them to the door an hour and a half later. This time she took a tract about death and promised to read it. She seemed especially delighted with the Gospel of John that Cindy gave her.

"You will come back when you can, won't you?" she invited. She seemed to sincerely want to talk more about the truths she had learned.

The woman said that "her conscience was her Bible."

The Apostle Paul said that those who have no law, "are a law to themselves, who show the work of the law written in their hearts, their conscience also bearing witness" (Romans 2:14-15).

The girls thought about the two women, the woman who showed mild interest looked away from them during their time of need. The "atheist," hard as she seemed, had in her heart the knowledge of right and wrong, which God used to bring more light on her path.

Looking Inward: We chafe at the price we sometimes have to pay to be useful to God. Perhaps it won't be the bite of a vicious dog, but there may be a personal price to pay for faithful witnessing.

Looking Outward: We look on the outside; God looks on the inside. We see "an atheist." God sees someone with a sensitive conscience, accepting all the truth she knows, ready to respond to the gospel when it comes her way.

W.W.
Operation Mobilization (OM)

Nine

The Little Boats
of the Dyaks

Borneo

Jesus alone can make atonement because He is the atonement—the at-one-ment of God and man. —Bonville Beytagh, *A Glimpse of Glory*

Each year, the people of a village called Anik in Borneo prepare a small boat. It is a solemn and fearful occasion, for much depends on how the boat will carry its cargo down river.

When the craftsmen finish the boat, they hand it to the elders of the town. As the entire population of Anik watch, an elder carefully selects two chickens from the village flock. He checks carefully to see the chickens are clean and healthy. Then he slays one of the chickens and sprinkles its blood along the shore. The second chicken is tied up carefully and placed alive on one end of the little boat.

Another elder brings a small lantern, secures it to the other end of the boat and lights it. At that point every person in the village walks by and places an invisible object on the ship.

What are they placing there? one may ask. "*Dosaku*," they would answer which means "our sin." When every villager has placed his *dosa* on the little boat, the village elders, with great ceremony, lift the boat, wade out into the river, and place it in the water.

Then the people wait . . . and watch. Every eye is on the little boat as it drifts downstream. Fears rage within each heart, hoping that the little boat won't drift toward shore and lodge there. Sad to say, that would mean that their sins were not carried away as they hoped—at least until next year when the ritual is repeated.

On and on it drifts, and finally only the tiny lantern can be seen, the form of the boat being swallowed up in the darkness. Then the light can no more be seen as the boat drifts around the bend of the river.

A cry of joy goes up, *"Selamat! Selamat!"* meaning "We're safe!, we're safe!" This might be compared to a high priest of ancient Israel who shouted the cry of *"Shalom! Shalom!"* translated "Peace! Peace!"

But the Dyaks feel safe only until next year.

One wonders where such a custom arose. Was it a form of a similar Jewish ritual where the priest selected two goats? One was to be slain on the altar. After the people had laid their hands on the other goat, symbolically placing their sins on it, the goat would be driven off into the wilderness. This represented the bearing away the sins of the people, much like the Dyak's boat.

Which one really could bear away sin? Neither! The writer of the book of Hebrews said of the Jewish ritual: "But in those sacrifices there is a reminder of sins every year. For it is not possible that the blood of bulls and goats could take away sins. .. By that will we have been sanctified through the offering of the body of Jesus Christ once for all" (Hebrews 10:3-10).

Perhaps one day all people such as the Dyaks, who look to ancient forms and shadows, will find the reality of sins forgiven and life eternal provided by the once-for-all sacrifice of Christ.

Looking Inward: The world has a multitude of substitutes for the truth. The worst is lingering hope in our hearts that we can, by some extra effort, make ourselves fit for heaven apart from God's grace. Our foolish search causes us at many stages of our journey to miss the full joy of knowing God loves and forgives us because of Christ.

Looking Outward: Often we take for granted that the blood of Jesus spanned a tremendous chasm to bring us to God. We lose sight of the millions who still look to the blood of chickens and goats, of little boats with twinkling lanterns floating down rivers. In vain they hope to find *Selamat!* or *Shalom,*when Jesus, the Prince of Peace, has already paid the full price of peace for us all.

W.W.
Story adapted from *Eternity in Their Hearts,* Don Richardson, Regal Books, 1981, used by permission.

Ten

Florin's Red Badge
Of Courage

Romania

The world is in constant conspiracy against the brave. It's the age-old struggle—the roar of the crowd on one side and the voice of your conscience on the other. —General Douglas MacArthur, (Public statement on his 84th and last birthday)

I met Florin the morning he was to go with me to a small village in the northwest corner of Romania, several years ago—before the barbed wire and the cement of the Iron Curtain came down. I was in Romania doing research for a book. My contact person in the nearby city of Cluj spoke very little English, so he arranged for his relative, twenty-year-old Florin to accompany us that day.

He seemed shy at first, nervously combing dark red hair as his cousin introduced him. Soon he began to warm up, showing an engaging smile. Striking blue eyes began to twinkle, and he seemed to relax when he realized I could understand his English. I knew immediately I would like him.

He told me he worked as an apprentice elevator repairman. His rough chapped hand, reaching out to shake mine, told me how hard he worked for his living

The quaint old city of Cluj was now ringed by hundreds of tall, monstrously ugly and poorly constructed apartment buildings, a part of the communists' resettlement plan. Farm villages by the hundreds had been torn down, forcing people to move into cities to work in inefficient factories. These huge apartment buildings were constantly in need of elevator repairs.

"At least your job is secure," I suggested.

"I am never sure about that," he said. "My manager knows now that I am a Christian." Florin pointed to a little red New Testament he carried in his shirt pocket. He said he carried it there, over his heart, since the day he received Christ several years before. Displaying so openly the Scriptures was his red badge of courage, in a country whose government vowed several decades before to wipe out Christianity. Though he might never shed blood for his faith, it would certainly cost him something.

"My manager has said he could never promote me unless I give up my Christianity," he continued.

I wondered about how his spending the day with me, an American Christian writing about Christianity in Romania, might be putting him further in harm's way.

"No, I didn't have to tell them what I was doing today. I said only that I wanted to visit some relatives in the village where we are going," he assured me. Then I realized that I had at least cost him one precious day of his short annual vacation. But somehow the look on his face told me it was part of a decision he had already made. I thought of the verse: "Though I walk in the midst of trouble, You will revive me. You will stretch out Your hand against the wrath of my enemies, and Your right hand will save me" (Psalm 138:7).

The village sat high on a hill above the main highway. We parked the car and walked up the steep and rocky unpaved road, accessible only by carts. Older men and women were dressed in costume one might have expected to see a century ago—bright colored native-woven scarves for the women and coarse homespun coats and pants for the men.

The village was perhaps two hundred thatched-roof buildings clustered around the hill, many of their mud brick walls still wearing the blue-tinted whitewash commonly used for centuries. Ancient stoves, lit to break the late afternoon chill, sent thin trails of smoke from ancient chimneys. Oxen-drawn plows were breaking the last furrows for garden plots. Bleating sheep and cows, banded with melodic bells, were returning across the hill, chased home by young boys and girls. The April sun cast peaceful shadows across the valley. The village, untouched by the culture the communist leaders tried to impose on it, seemed light years removed from oppressive ethos of the city below.

Florin took me first to a crumbling building, the Baptist Church. Built of cement-plastered mud brick, it was plain looking except for the tilting wooden cross atop its rusty metal roof. The building was, among other things, a monument to faithful believers who stood for years against the pressures of first the Orthodox Church and later the Marxist indoctrinators, who vowed to one day crush them.

Behind the little church was the community building, once a synagogue until first the Nazis and then the communists took over. Florin pointed out a small graveyard behind the building. Several dark gray stones with Hebrew inscriptions now barely legible, tilted sadly among the weedy plot.

"All but one of the children of this family died in Auschwitz," Florin told me. Perhaps young men, no older than Florin, had laid down their lives in a foreign land, simply because someone said they were foreigners who didn't belong in that country.

The quiet afternoon was suddenly broken by a Russian-built MiG fighter jet, streaking over the mountain range east of us, the same mountains over which Trajan's army had marched centuries ago to conquer this ancient land of Dacia. How many young Romans Florin's age, miles from their homeland, had died to fulfill the wishes of their despotic emperor to conquer this land. Were they afraid, or were they courageous, as Roman soldiers were supposed to be? I wondered. And did these Roman soldiers believe in what they were doing, and were they willing to die for it? And what of the young jet pilot streaking overhead, up there doing the bidding of his government many miles to the east of us. Did he really believe in what he was doing?

Later that afternoon, some of Florin's relatives from the village prepared a light meal for us—soup, boiled eggs, and thick unpasteurized milk. An ancient matriarch, in layers of frayed clothes, sat quietly in a corner, nubbing out dried corn by hand. Chickens walked over the doorstep inches behind me. The quiet pastoral kitchen made the oppressive, demanding government system seem miles and centuries away. But the hidden restraints were there, and there was a price to pay for challenging it. Nobody talked about it—even in the privacy of this home, but it was there, just out of sight.

As twilight faded, we thanked our gracious hosts and stumbled through the darkness down the twisting ox cart trail to my car parked at the foot of the hill.

Back in the city, Florin asked me not to take him directly to his home.

"Please let me out here. I can walk the few blocks to my home." He didn't want his neighbors to see him get out of a foreigner's car. In Romania, cars rented by people from capitalist countries bear easily recognized license numbers. I knew we were under constant surveillance by the police and informers.

Realizing I had already put my friend in enough jeopardy, I stopped on a quiet street corner, switched off the engine, and turned to my friend to say good-bye. Words of thanks seemed hopelessly inadequate. His last words to me before he hugged me tightly and slipped out into the night were unforgettable.

"Will you pray for me? Will you promise? No, it would be better if you didn't write to me. But pray. Each week I listen to the Bible studies from the radio broadcast coming from America. Those lessons are all I have to learn the Bible. Books are almost impossible to get here. We often have to meet in secret to study. I want to learn more about the Bible so I can help my people. God has put my country Romania so heavily on my heart! Please pray for me that I may learn how to be useful."

I thought of the pressures on him and the price he was paying—even for that little red New Testament he carried in his pocket, which was all he had to encourage him through dark days. I thought also of how hard it would be to tell people who wear no badge of courage, people whose lives show they have never had a price to pay for what they believe—people who live in their own comfortable land and who seek no other?

I will never know about Trajan's soldiers who once walked those hills. Nor will I likely meet the MiG pilot who streaked over us that afternoon — what they thought, what they believed. But I realized that afternoon I had been in the presence of a courageous young man who knew what he believed and was ready to lay down his life for it.

Looking Inward: Florin's photograph over my desk makes me ask myself a question every day as I pray for him: Am I just "taking it easy" today? Or is my faith in Christ costing me something — time, energy, money?

Looking Outward: The indisputable presentation of the gospel we can make to a world grown cold with skepticism is the way we show our love for God — loving one another sacrificially, allowing our faith to cost us something.

W.W.
Romanian Missionary Society (RMS)

Eleven

Gloria
I Will Fear No Evil

Bolivia

Despise evil and ungodliness, but not men of ungodliness and evil. These, understand. —William Saroyan, *The Time of Your Life*, Act 1.

Classes were over for the evening at the Bolivian Evangelical University. Gloria's eyes were glued to an adjoining classroom building, waiting for Luis to appear.

They were two busy students, with very little time for each other. They both looked forward to a life of ministry together. But tonight Gloria and Luis had a more pressing mission. They were making plans to talk to Sophia, Luis's mother, to announce their engagement.

Gloria was patting her long black hair and straightening her red flowered skirt just as Luis, textbooks in hand, rushed out of the classroom in her direction. His face seemed to glow at the sight of her. In the few moments they had together, they decided that tomorrow they would break the news.

Laughing and talking excitedly, they drove off the next day in Gloria's car toward Sophia's house on the other side of Santa Cruz. Winding through narrow streets, dodging ox carts and bicycles, they made their way through the sweltering heat to Luis's family home.

Sophia met them at the door, a stern look on her face.

"This is Gloria," Luis said proudly.

No answer.

Gloria smiled at the woman, now glaring at her. "My son has told me all about you," she said gruffly. "I do not want him to marry you."

Luis and Gloria stood in shock, unable to say a word.

"Now go away! I don't want to see you again. You're not worthy of such a fine young man as my son, and you shall not marry my Luis. Luis, you are not to see Gloria again."

Gloria's joy vanished. She had prayed so much about the wedding! *What was God doing with them to allow this to happen?* she wondered. Slowly Gloria and Luis retraced their route to the university, hardly speaking on the way.

The next days were hard for both of them. Yet, after many long talks they decided not to give up their plans to be married, despite Sophia's objections.

Several weeks later a very strange thing happened. Sophia showed up at the seminary asking to see Gloria. Evidently she had remembered Gloria's car from their visit several weeks before. Realizing her son would not give up his plans to marry Gloria, Sophia decided to take another approach.

"I need to make a trip," she said to Gloria. "Will you take me in your car?"

"Why, yes," Gloria responded without a second of hesitation. *When she gets to know me, she'll see what a good wife I will make for her son*, she thought.

On the day they had agreed upon, Gloria drove to Sophia's house, and they were off. Sophia pointed out directions for Gloria. After a short drive, they arrived at a very ordinary looking house surrounded as usual by a high brick wall, topped by jagged broken glass to discourage robbers. Sophia banged on the back iron gate, until someone opened it and let them in.

Sophia led the way across the yard and into the darkened house. As soon as Gloria saw the woman inside, she understood the reason for the trip. Across the room sat an old woman, her dark evil-looking eyes seeming to pierce through Gloria.

She was a witch. Sophia had brought her to this evil place so the witch could put a hex on her.

As a young university student, Gloria felt poorly prepared to face the evil onslaught. She wasn't a Christian when she arrived at the university. All she knew about God and the Bible she had learned in the compulsory Bible courses and chapel messages. But she had heard more than once about the power of prayer and how she could, at any time, talk to God.

Oppression hung over the dark room. Shaking with fear, Gloria lifted her face upward and breathed a silent prayer: *Oh God, save me!*

It appeared a heavy weight was lifted, and the room seemed somehow lighter, less fearful. Gloria's trembling ceased and she stared back at the witch, unblinking.

Then the witch croaked hoarsely at her, "Get out of here!"

Sophia protested. "We can't go yet. You must do what I paid you to do. If you need more money, I'll get it for you!"

"I can't do it for you," the witch replied. "There is something within her spirit that my spirit cannot touch."

Gloria then bolted for the car, Sophia right behind her. Driving as fast as she dared, she returned to Sophia's house, let her out of the car, and then drove straight to the university to find Luis and some of her teachers. Breathlessly, she explained to them what had happened. The words of the Apostle John suddenly took on meaning it never before had for her: "You are of God, little children, and have overcome them, because He who is in you is greater than he who is in the world" (1 John 4:4).

Something else happened that day, Gloria and Luis learned later—something that would change Sophia in many ways. The result was, first, that Gloria and Luis were married with her blessing. More important, Sophia wanted Gloria's God to be her God, so she prayed to receive Christ as her Savior.

Looking Inward: It is God's goodness that occasionally casts us into deep waters so we cry out to him for help. Many hours of each day other things fill our horizons. How slow we are to learn! How much we need to pray daily the words of the hymn by Annie Hawkes:
"I need Thee every hour, Most gracious Lord;
No tender voice like Thine can peace afford."

Looking Outward: The words we say to others, the truths we teach about God and His saving power, the prayers we utter that others might grow in the grace and knowledge of our Lord Jesus Christ— these may be the weapons God will use to strengthen people like Gloria in their time of deep spiritual need. How glad her teachers must have been for the opportunity God had given them to prepare Gloria for that moment she stood in the presence of Satan's power.

W.W.
World Gospel Mission (WGM)

Twelve

A Visit with
Madame Goetz

France

Obedience is not slavery: but ordered liberty. —Gilbert
Shaw, *Perfection*

Abe and Mary Kroeker, Bible Literature Fellowship
missionaries, finished breakfast in their tiny apartment and
huddled for another moment in front of the glowing coal stove.
Pushing back the lace curtain, Abe looked again at the cold rain
falling, sighed his disappointment, and returned to the stove. He
and Mary still felt exhausted from their recent move to this new
apartment outside Metz. It was ideally located, but all the painting
and wall-papering had been a much larger task than they had
anticipated. Seeing the cold rain falling, he was tempted to forget
about their planned trip that morning.

Since the three young ladies from the Goetz family had brought
their mother, Madame Goetz, to the Bible study Abe and Mary
conducted, and after their interesting conversation with the older
woman, she had often been on both their minds. On several
occasions during their family prayers together, the Lord had
brought Madame Goetz to one of their minds, and they would
pray for her.

During the conversation several weeks before, Madame Goetz
had invited Abe and Mary to visit in her home across town in the
small suburb of Devant-les-Ponts. At the time, and several times
since then, they had wondered if she sincerely wanted a visit or
was just being polite for the kindness they had showed her
daughters.

The more they prayed for Madame Goetz, the more certain Abe and Mary felt that they should take her at her word and visit her. Abe remembered how interested she had seemed when he had been teaching from the passage in Romans: "The righteousness of God which is through faith in Jesus Christ to all and on all who believe" (3:22). Later Abe had explained that salvation was by grace alone, emphasizing the verse, "And if by grace, then it is no longer of works, otherwise, grace is no longer grace."

Madame Goetz had become uneasy at that point, and later reminded the Kroekers that she had been a religious woman all her life, attended church, and gave money to charity. She seemed to have many questions, and it was then that she had invited them to visit her one day. It was to follow up on that slightly opened door that Abe and Mary wanted to try to enter.

"We should go," Mary said, now at the window watching the rain come down. It would mean waiting in the rain for a bus to take them to the downtown cathedral where they would wait for another bus to Devant-les-Ponts.

"Then let's go," Abe responded.

Meanwhile across town, Madame Goetz kissed her daughters, one by one, as they left their quiet home in Devant-les-Ponts. Recently there was a tenderness in their voices she couldn't understand. Since they had been attending Bible classes, she noticed the girls seemed much closer and more loving to each other, but they showed an affectionate sadness toward her.

Something has happened to them at those Bible classes, she thought. *They have changed so much. Perhaps that couple I invited will come someday as they promised and explain it to me. But certainly not today,* she sighed as she pushed back the curtain in her kitchen and saw the cold rain falling.

When she and her daughters had returned from the Bible class, she had asked one of them to find the Bible verses that Abe had read—the verses that troubled her. Her daughter found the passage and placed a marker there, perhaps hoping her mother would return to it and read it over again.

The dreary rain made the whole house seem dark. Finding her daughter's Bible, Madame Goetz brought it to the window. She pushed back the curtains and read the words again: "For if Abraham was justified by works, he has something of which to boast, but not before God . . . Abraham believed God, and it was accounted to him for righteousness" (Romans 4:2-3).

It seemed so strange, especially to one who had tried to live properly, to attend church, and to do good works to approach God.

To Madame Goetz, at that moment God seemed strangely far away, as someone she should know but as a stranger standing at a distance, unapproaching and unapproachable. She would have to ask the Kroekers about these thoughts—if they ever came.

Perhaps she had misread the Kroekers. They had seemed so warm toward her, caring. It was unusual for people to show that much love to her. Several times during the past few days she had wondered, when her thoughts had turned toward God, if they weren't actually praying for her. She had heard of such things. But perhaps she was wrong, since they hadn't come as promised.

The buzzer at the front door sounded.

Who would this be—on such a cold rainy morning? she asked herself. She opened the door and saw Abe and Mary, smiling, water dripping from their coats and umbrellas.

"What a wonderful surprise!" she said to them. Ushering them inside and putting away their rain gear, she invited them into her parlor. Then she prepared hot drinks for them.

After they had settled with their cups of coffee, Abe began the conversation. "Madame Goetz, you may know about the decisions your daughters, Odette, Denise, and Solange, have made about their lives. But may I ask you a question? Are you certain about your relationship to God? Do you have the assurance of salvation?"

"Monsieur Kroeker," she said, "that is exactly what I've been asking myself for some time. But, first, may I ask you a question?"

"Of course," he said.

"Have you not thought a lot about me lately? Have you perhaps been praying for me?

Mary and Abe looked at each other in surprise. "Why, yes, we have, Madame"

"I knew it!" she said, "I felt it!"

The rest of the conversation was one of questions and answers. At the end, Madame Goetz clasped her hands and bowed in prayer—not to a Stranger far away but to God her Friend, who loved her very much.

She could hardly wait for the girls to return home that evening. She met them at the door. "Odette, Denise, Solange, tell me, do you notice anything different?"

The girls looked at the radiant face of their mother, then at each other in surprise. Odette spoke first. "Mother! You are saved!"

"Yes," and after explaining some new truths the Kroekers had left with her, she pointed to her heart. "The Holy Spirit lives here now," she said, reaching for the outstretched arms of her daughters.

Mary and Abe were floating as they rode the bus back home through the rainy streets of Metz. It had seemed such a sacrifice to leave the warmth of the glowing coal stove. They thought of the psalmist's words: "He who continually goes forth weeping, bearing seed for sowing, shall doubtless come again with rejoicing, bringing his sheaves with him" (Psalm 126:6). The warmth in their hearts made it all seem worthwhile.

Looking Inward: Obedience always has a price tag. But the blessings God returns for our obedience makes such a life of dedication a bargain at any price.

Looking Outward: It always seems warm inside, but outside the world is cold, needy, and waiting for answers. Only those who venture out into the cold will ever understand true comfort and feel the heartwarming Breath of God flowing through their lives.

W.W.
Bible Literature Fellowship (BLF)

Thirteen

Telephone Directories from Seventy-five Countries

India

Never close your lips to those to whom you have opened your heart. —Charles Dickens

---

Mobin Khan was warned not to go to the Maldive Islands. The people there are all Muslims. The government is hostile to Christians. Mobin took his Indian passport to be safe, because many Indians from south India holiday in the Maldives. But when he arrived, he wrote his U.S. address on the Immigration Card by mistake.

The Maldive authorities singled him out of all the passengers, 90 percent of whom were Indians. One official asked, "Where are you staying? Why is your return flight to America when your passport is Indian?" His pockets were filled with gospel tracts because he knew that the customs officials never checked pockets. He would have been arrested if caught bringing in Christian literature. Yet, during the long interrogation, no one thought to ask him about all the coats he was wearing.

After being released, Mobin rested and prayed in his room. Then he went for a walk and placed gospel tracts in the public bathroom. After half an hour, he walked by again and discovered that none remained. He replaced them again. At the post office he stuffed tracts into the open postal boxes when no one was watching.

Next he decided to contact a government official. This time Mobin would wear his American hat, because he could probably find one official who would make time to visit with an American.

After several phone calls, Mobin was invited to visit the minister of education. Mobin saw a telephone directory on the official's desk. Since the island was small, most people didn't use a telephone. They walked to each other's homes and offices to converse.

Mobin asked, "Can I take the telephone directory?"

The government official asked, "Why do you want it?"

He replied, "Because it is my hobby to collect telephone directories."

The minister of education called the telephone company and asked for a new directory. Mobin offered to pick it up. When he arrived, the receptionist wrote something down in Arabic.

Mobin asked, "Why do you write in Arabic? Why don't you write in your own script?

She replied, "Because you couldn't understand my script."

"Can you teach me?"

"It will take three months."

"I only have seven days."

"Then, I will try. Come to my house this evening."

After talking to her a while, Mobin discovered that she was a single, divorced girl in her twenties.

"Why are you divorced? Did your husband run away with another woman better looking?" asked Mobin.

She looked surprised. "How did you know that?"

"Isn't this country a Muslim country? Aren't you a Muslim? How could he run away?"

"No, nobody is Muslim. Everyone claims to be Muslim, but people aren't practicing their religion."

"Is there something wrong with Islam?"

She looked shocked, "Aren't you Muslim?"

"I used to be." Then Mobin told her his testimony.

"I was born and brought up in a Sunni Muslim family in Banaras, India. When I was five years old, I was taught how to read the Koran in the Arabic language." he began.

In India, Mobin had to learn Arabic in order to read the Koran. The Muslims believe that their god Allah understands only Arabic. Mobin learned to read the Koran from beginning to end.

Later Mobin was sent to a Muslim discipleship program. While studying there, he learned about God, God's holy angels, and God's prophets. He learned that God sent four holy books to mankind: Tawratt (Torah) which was sent to the prophet Moses; Zabur

(Psalms) which was sent to the prophet David; Injil (Gospels) which was sent to prophet Jesus; and Koran which was sent to prophet Mohammed.

Mobin asked his teacher, "You have taught us the fourth book so far. When are you going to teach us the other three books?"

The teacher answered, "The other books are with the Jews and Christians."

"Would you go to a Christian and a Jew and get these books for me to read?" he asked his teacher. "After all, they are God's books, and I want to read God's books."

To that the teacher replied, "The Jews and the Christians got together and changed the books. You cannot read them."

But the desire to read what was missing from the Holy Books never left Mobin's mind.

Mobin believed what his teacher told him at age five in the Muslim school, but at the age of six he started attending the secular school where his friends were mostly Hindus. One day he told his friends, "You'll go to hell." He had been taught that all the people of the world who weren't Muslims would go to hell and that only Muslims go to heaven.

His school friends acted shocked when he made his bold statement, so he asked his friends what they believed. One replied, "All Muslims will go to hell because they eat beef—our holy cows."

Mobin began to question—to wonder why he would go to heaven just because his parents were Muslim. As he grew up, he became an atheist and decided that all religion was just man-made.

At fifteen he joined the Indian army and went to a training camp. There he became friends with an officer who he later discovered was a Christian, although at first he didn't realize it.

One evening the officer began sharing the gospel with Mobin. The officer said, "War is going to break out with Pakistan anytime. You might be called to the front and killed by the Pakistan Air Force. If you die, you will go to hell. If I die, I will go to heaven because I believe in Jesus."

Mobin was not ready to accept the officer's logic. He had heard the same things about Islam in his childhood that now the officer was saying about Christianity. He didn't believe the officer, so he walked out of the room.

The officer began praying for Mobin's salvation.

Mobin went to bed with his mind churning. Something the man had said intrigued him, and the next morning Mobin returned to the officer's room and asked, "Could you share with me once again what we discussed last night." They made plans to meet later.

The officer gave Mobin a New Testament and said, "This book has all the answers you need to know. Take it and read it, but don't begin with Matthew, Mark, and Luke. Read the Book of John first.

"I'll read it," Mobin agreed. At the time, he had no idea that the New Testament was part of the Bible. If he had known, he never would have read it. The beautiful cover said, "The New Testament." It didn't say Bible. Mobin had no idea he was reading a Christian book.

He opened it and read John 1:1: "In the beginning was the Word, and the Word was with God, and the Word was God" His favorite subject was philosophy, and this book sounded like Indian philosophy, so he kept reading.

Day after day he continued to read, not fully understanding all he read. Soon he reached Romans 5:8: "But God demonstrates His own love toward us, in that while we were still sinners Christ died for us." His eyes were opened, and he began to grasp the significance of the life, death, and resurrection of Jesus Christ.

He then faced the problem of telling his father that he had become a Christian believer. When his family found out he was serious in his belief and that he was practicing the Christian faith, they were extremely upset. His father insisted that Mobin go to a mosque with the family, but Mobin refused. As a result he had to leave his home. He was still a minor then. Two years later his father came searching for him. Mobin was afraid to go back home, fearing his father would beat him. Christians friends would hide him as he moved around from town to town. He wrote to his family every week from a different location, but he never heard back from them because he never gave an address. The Christian pastor in his town kept in touch with him, but he never went to Mobin's home, fearing Mobin's father would have him arrested.

After a while, Mobin realized that his family was suffering as well as the pastor who had encouraged him. Back home, his father must have seen his dedication and gave up trying to bring him back into Islam. In fact, he helped Mobin get an education.

It was a hard decision to leave home at such a young age, and there was a price to pay. But God honored him for it.

In college, Mobin was known to go from room to room with Bible studies, anxious to share his faith wherever he could.

Years later, the Lord brought Mobin Khan to Fuller Seminary in Pasadena, California. One day, out of curiosity he opened a local telephone directory and saw ten Khan families in the directory. He thought about calling them, but decided they would be filled with questions and doubt about his religion. They might ask, "What are you doing here? Then he thought of the idea to send them a tract in the mail. That way they could receive the gospel but would never know who had sent it. So he sent each of them a tract.

In 1979 he decided to expand his ministry to all the Muslim names listed in the Pasadena directory. He started marking all the names and discovered there were 1400. Daily commuters came from Los Angeles and the San Fernando Valley to Fuller Seminary. Mobin realized that the entire metropolitan Los Angeles area had a large number of Muslims living in the three counties. He obtained telephone directories for all the cities and started mailing tracts to all of the Muslim names. Now the ministry has expanded to more than a hundred countries. One of their main methods of reaching people worldwide is still telephone directories.

When Mobin visits foreign cities, as he was doing that day in the Maldive Islands, he still tells people, "I collect telephone directories. Do you have one I can take home with me?"

Looking Inward: A small New Testament brought light into Mobin's life. Light dispels darkness, but the powers of darkness try to fight back. It took courage to stand against his family's religion, but true light in the heart can give clear direction and encouragement.

Looking Outward: Light in our hearts, if it is true light, will shine out to reach others. Mobin learned at an early age that Christians have something that other religious groups don't possess. That something is Jesus Christ. The best witness we can give to others is for them to see the light of Christ shining within us.

S.T.O.
Christian Missions in Many Lands

Fourteen

Jaki
Counting Words

Papua
New Guinea

When God wants an impossible task done, He chooses an impossible person. —Chuck Colson

---

Jaki Parlier sat, resting her back on the trunk of a banana tree. "What a gorgeous day for relaxing with a good book," she said out loud. Thinking herself alone, she was startled by a voice behind her.

"Greetings," said Raka grinning down at her. Glancing at the book he asked, "What are you doing?"

"Uh-oh," Jaki thought, wondering how to say "I'm reading" in the Managalasi language.

After some thought she chose the closest idiom she could find. "I'm counting words."

"What words?" he asked, taking the book from her hands. "Where are they?" His eyes moved curiously from Jaki to the book, then back to her again.

"It's, uh . . . the words we . . . uh, . . . say with our mouths," she stammered.

Jaki and her husband, Jim Parlier, were new Wycliffe Bible Translators, assigned to this small village in Papua New Guinea, where they had come to learn the language and eventually to translate the Scriptures. Jaki was still struggling to communicate with her Managalasi friends. The words she wanted to say weren't coming out right. Frustrated, she watched him stare at the book, trying to see the words.

"There," Jaki said, pointing to the fine print. "I look at these marks, and I can hear my language."

Raka squinted at the strange marks, trying to make sense of them, then held the book up towards the sun to get a better look. Finally he put the book next to his ear and waited, as if the words would speak to him if he listened long enough.

Suddenly Jaki realized that Raka didn't know what a book was. Probably no one else in the village did either.

Raka handed the book back to Jaki and went on his way. His response to the words on the page that he couldn't hear pointed out the need to get a book in the Managalasi language into print. Slumping there under the banana tree, her head in her hands, Jaki felt discouraged because of how little of the language she knew. She wondered how she would ever get a book into print that people like Raka could learn to read.

Returning to her desk, Jaki picked up the word file containing all the Managalasi words she had collected to use as a dictionary. Doggedly, she went through each three-by-five card and made lists of the short words. Next she chose words that had the same kinds of syllables. Hours passed as she agonized over how to make a reader. Finally she came up with a story about "father" which read: "This is father. Father can see. Father sees pigs. Father sees coconuts. Father sees yams."

The first Managalasi book was underway! In her excitement, Jaki barely noticed that the kerosene lamp had started flickering. Her husband had gone to bed hours ago.

The next morning Jaki finished the story about father and illustrated each page. Father became a stick figure wearing a G-string. After laboriously making six copies by hand, she felt ready to round up the book-starved men. She ran to the village and yelled loudly, "All the men, come! Come and hear my talk."

A few faces peered out from doorways. Several children ran frightened into their houses, but no one rushed out to join Jaki.

Patiently she leaned against a coconut tree and waited. A few young girls sauntered over and sat down. They looked at Jaki and giggled. She turned and faced the other direction, ignoring them. She wanted to interest the men in reading—the important, prestigious men. Learning to read must be thought of as a special privilege in the community.

Eventually most of the men gathered around the missionary woman. She held up the books and tried to convey how wonderful it was to count words. She wondered if they understood her chopped-up Managalasi. Although she felt like a stammering two-year-old, she plunged on. However, most of the men looked away as if embarrassed by what she said. When she finished, silence hung like a thick cloud over the audience.

Trying to sound carefree, Jaki asked, "Who wants to learn to count words?"

The entire group evaded her stare, as if she had offended them. Finally one man spoke up, "We have to work in our gardens. Will learning to read help our gardens grow?"

Unprepared for this question, Jaki wasn't sure how to answer. "You . . . uh . . . have to learn so you can . . . uh . . . read God's Book and . . ." Suddenly she stopped. She could tell it was no use. Not one of them cared about God—yet.

The group began to leave, taking the last of Jaki's enthusiasm with them. Suppressing an urge to fling the readers into the wind, she headed home clutching her precious hand-made books under her arm.

That night she flopped down on her bed, defeated. She shouted, "Lord, why did you send us here? You knew these people wouldn't be interested in reading." All she could think of at the moment was returning to the United States and relaxing somewhere on a soft couch, speaking her own language, blissfully unaware of failure.

Sun streaming in her window awoke Jaki the next morning. Still depressed, she gazed out the window and noticed the chubby young girl, Sonalu, hanging out clothes. An idea flashed in her mind. She yelled, "Sonalu, come here. You're going to learn to count words."

Jaki dressed quickly and set up two kerosene drums. "Sit down," she said, patting the drum. Not wasting a moment, she opened the reader and began instructing, "This is `ma,'" Jaki said pointing to the syllable. "Now, you say it."

"Ma!" she yelled back so loudly that Jaki jumped, dropping the book. Sonalu laughed hysterically. "Sorry," she mumbled, still laughing. She covered her mouth trying to lock the laughter inside; only it got worse. Soon Jaki was laughing with her, and both were wiping tears from their eyes.

Settling down they resumed class, and Sonalu learned to read two pages. The reader was working! Long after class, Sonalu sat reading the same two pages over and over. Finally she went home, clutching the book proudly in her hand.

Early the next morning she was back with two giggly girls, the ones Jaki had ignored two days before. "They want to learn, too," she explained.

Jaki was at first reluctant, but she put readers into their hands and showed them how to turn pages. The girls learned quickly, going through the readers faster than Jaki dreamed possible. Responding to their enthusiasm, Jaki created a second reader, then a third. After three months, the girls could read anything Jaki placed before them.

Some time later on a Sunday afternoon, Jim and Jaki strolled up to the village. A crowd stood in front of Sonalu's house, staring down at something. The silence was overwhelming.

Anxiously Jaki nudged her way through the crowd with Jim close behind. Reaching the center, Jaki realized what drew the stunned, silent crowd. There on a banana leaf sat three girls reading Genesis aloud, pretending not to notice they had the attention of the entire village.

Jaki looked at the faces in the crowd. They wore expressions of profound wonder and respect. Jaki, who had been so discouraged and ready to go home, stood watching girls, who a few months ago didn't know how to hold a book, reading God's Word to the whole village.

Looking Inward: Sometimes we are fearful that we won't be able to accomplish all we believe God wants us to do. If we depend on our own strength, we won't. Yet, God often uses ordinary people, depending on Him, to accomplish the most astonishing tasks.

Looking Outward: Sometimes we mistakenly think that the only way to reach people is through the most prestigious community leaders. Knowledge forced on people through human effort accomplishes little. Our responsibility is to share the Word wherever it will be received and then leave the results to God. He has promised, "So shall My word be that goes forth from My mouth; it shall not return to Me void, but it shall accomplish what I please, and it shall prosper in the thing for which I sent it" (Isaiah 55:11).

S.T.O.
Wycliffe Bible Translators

Fifteen

Archbishop Janani Luwum
The Empty Grave

Uganda

Evil can never be undone, but only purged and redeemed.
—Dorothy Sayers

The lid of the coffin creaked slowly open. In the half-light, a group of believers watched breathlessly as one of their number pried at the lid of the rough, wooden casket. Gradually the rusty nails gave way. The group gasped. The flickering gleam of the hurricane lamp revealed a body clad in a priest's purple robe, covered with blood-stains.

"It really is the archbishop," said a middle-aged woman, peering at the familiar figure. Tears welled up in her eyes and ran down her ebony face.

"And look," said another woman, leaning over her shoulder, "there are bullet holes in his body."

The small group knew they were risking their lives by trying to examine the body of this martyr. His arms were badly skinned, his rings had been stolen, and his shoes were gone.

The woman who identified Janani Luwum, the Anglican archbishop, stood over the casket and prayed softly, "Thank you, Jesus, for Janani," her hand tenderly caressing the lifeless form. "For through his life and death, I know many will come to You."

Did she understand something others might not have seen at that dark moment? Perhaps she was referring to what Paul meant when he spoke of his hardships, "the things which happened to me have actually turned out for the furtherance of the gospel" (Philippians 1:12).

The priest's body had been found in Mucwini, a Ugandan village near the Sudan border of the East Acholi District. He was one of the many victims of Idi Amin, the despot who, between 1971 and 1979, went on an orgy of bloodshed. An estimated 500,000 Ugandan countrymen were shot, tortured, and battered to death—many of them, possibly 300,000, Ugandan Christians.

Idi Amin, on what he claimed was direct orders of Allah, closed most of the churches in his country. He wrote himself into church history on February 17, 1977, by personally shooting Anglican Archbishop Janani Luwum, as the cleric knelt before him.

Luwum was accused by Amin of being involved in a plot against him and was brought into Amin's office. During the interrogation, the archbishop refused to sign a confession. He was ordered to lie on the floor. His cassock was pulled up, and two soldiers in turn whipped him.

After the beating, Luwum began praying quietly, his words barely a whisper. This was the final straw for Amin. Shouting obscenities, angrily and wildly, he struck the archbishop. Then he bellowed at an Acholi soldier "Kill him! Kill him!"

The shaking Ancholi soldier, who came from the same tribe as the archbishop, aimed his gun and shot the archbishop in the groin. With that, Amin drew his pistol and fired into Luwum's face. The bullet struck the archbishop in the mouth as he was lowering his head.

Amin, suddenly shocked by what he had done, reached for the telephone and said to someone on the other end: "I have lost my temper. I have shot the archbishop. Do something."

A "road accident" was staged, and the world was told that the archbishop and two government ministers, who were also killed, had died while trying to escape.

Amin would not allow a funeral service to take place at Janani's cathedral that stood atop Namirembe Hill. So the funeral took place in his home village of Mucwinmi, conducted by Archdeacon Kesoloni Oni, assisted by three other local clergymen. Despite the danger from Amin's troops, believers arrived in droves.

"The church was full," recalled the Right Reverend Gideon Oboma, Assistant Bishop of Northern Uganda. "The people were not afraid of the danger and were even preaching to the soldiers. They had said to themselves, 'If this is to be the time of death, let us also die. But if this is to be the time to stay and live on, we will be a strong Christian witness.'

"And witness they did. For one whole month, a group of believers kept vigil at the unmarked grave, over which they put a grass cover.

"They sang and thanked God for Janani's life. They slept in the open. Day and night they stayed at the grave, with the local Christians bringing food and drink to sustain them."

And while these brave men and women were risking their lives in memory of their beloved archbishop, the government-controlled newspaper, *Voice of Uganda*, published a call for Amin to be made emperor and proclaimed him "Son of God."

The senseless killings continued for two more years, until Amin was driven out of his country by the Tanzanian army to seek refuge first in Libya as a guest of Colonel Muammar Gadhafi, Chairman of Libya's Revolutionary Council and later in Saudi Arabia.

The founder and international director of ASSIST, Dan Wooding, was in Uganda where he heard this story just days after Amin fled the country. Attending a service in a Kampala church, he was surprised by the response from believers there. "They were holding a thanksgiving worship service to celebrate their liberation." But it was another part of the service that moved him most. "What was so incredible was that these people who had lost so much began to pray that Idi Amin would find Christ," Wooding reported. "There was no call for retribution, but just for his salvation."

Looking Inward: When we are wronged, we often want to get even with those who wronged us. We cry for revenge, but Jesus instructed his followers to "bless those who curse you, and pray for those who spitefully use you . . . and your reward will be great, and you will be sons of the Highest" (Luke 6:28,35).

Looking Outward: Nonbelievers are watching our reactions— especially when things don't go our way. They look to see if we will become angry and seek revenge, or if we will leave the judgment and recompense to God. Our response to such wrongdoing may be the only witness they will ever experience.

S.T.O.
Aid to Special Saints in Strategic Times (ASSIST)

Sixteen

Brother Jonah
The Empty Tank

China

There is in every miracle a silent chiding of the world, and a tacit reprehension of them who require, or who need miracles.
—John Donne, *Miracles*

Seventy-three-year-old Jonah, a native of Shanghai, filled his rucksack with Bibles and Christian literature and headed for the railway station. John Wesley said that the true itinerant evangelist needed only four qualities to be successful: "a back for any bed, a face for any weather, a stomach for any food, and strength for any work." Despite his age, Jonah was all that, and more.

At the station, he spent his last money on a ticket to a small town in Henan Province, twenty hours away. With no more money, he wouldn't eat for the next twenty hours. An American missionary with Open Doors wanted to go along to see what life was like for an aged itinerant evangelist in China today.

On the way Jonah told him why he was going there. "I received a request to preach the gospel in that town. Someone must have been converted while I was preaching somewhere else and told them about me. They are the only believers in a village of 500 people.

The third-class coach became his pulpit. With a radiant smile, he began to talk to his captive audience. Wedged in between two men, he began telling everyone his mission. A young family sat across from him.

Standing in the aisle were two young soldiers. One of them asked, "Old man, tell us why you seem so happy."

It was all the old man needed. "What do you think? What would be the happiest thing that could ever happen to you, and I'll tell you whether that has happened to me."

Answers from the people in the coach came quickly. One suggested "A big house would make me happy." Another said, "I just want to be loved by a beautiful and wonderful woman." Another said, "I'd like a passport to America." A soldier said he wanted to command the People's Liberation Army."

"I have all of these and more," Jonah said with a broad smile to the incredulous group around him.

"Let me see, now," he continued, "I have a mansion so large an emperor would be envious; I am loved devotedly by the most beautiful person in the world; I have the perfect freedom to go wherever I wish; and I happen to be a very close friend of the most powerful man on earth."

"In fact, I have received all of this from one person, and His name is Jesus Christ."

The sermon continued for the rest of the twenty hours on the train.

Finally, at the train station, Jonah looked more serious. "I think many of them are very near the kingdom." But then he spoke about the young man who had sat silently next to him in the coach. For some reason, Jonah had a bad feeling about him.

While they were standing there, a strange thing happened. A man walked up and pointed to three bicycles. He said, "Praise the Lord. God has answered my prayers," pointing to the bicycles. "The village where you are going is five hours away. I need two men to help me get the bicycles to the village."

Mounting the bicycles, they rode off. When they arrived at the village, it didn't take Jonah long to draw a crowd. Borrowing two metal pots he banged them together, assembled a crowd, and began preaching. For the next fifty minutes he preached about his namesake, Jonah, and his sermon of repentance to Nineveh. Several made decisions, so Jonah selected some of them to lead the group after he left. He gave them some Bibles, and he instructed them on how to keep the meetings going. He spent all afternoon with this smaller group.

As darkness fell someone rode a bicycle into the village shouting, "Someone from the Public Security Bureau is on his way here in a car."

"I knew it," Jonah said. "That young man I told you about has reported us. We must leave at once."

Jumping on their bicycles, they fled as fast as they could through the night to a nearby town to where a bus was leaving for Loyang, one of the major cities of Henan.

Climbing onto the bus five hours later, heavy with exhaustion from pedaling the bicycles through the night, they reached Henan.

It was months later before Jonah learned what had happened. The man whose bicycles they had used wrote Jonah to tell him the story. He said that on the way back to the village he passed the stalled car of the Public Security Officer, who had been following them, trying to catch up. The car was parked by the road, with three stranded occupants. A few weeks later, Jonah's friend heard the reason. He was attending a church meeting and heard a young man tell this story:

"I was a petrol (gasoline) pump assistant on duty one night when the local Public Security Bureau car drew in. The driver told me to fill the tank quickly as they were en route to arrest an itinerant evangelist who had just arrived that day by train. Hearing this, I stopped filling the tank and prayed that God would blind the driver's eyes from noticing. I'm sure it helped, for I have not heard of any arrest since."

What a joy it was for the young man to learn that he had in fact saved Jonah from being arrested! The Psalmist wrote, "For He shall give His angels charge over you, to keep you in all your ways" (Psalm 91:11). Sometimes His angels direct strange things to happen, even empty petrol tanks!

"Won't it be wonderful when we get to heaven and hear about all the other thousands of times God rescued us like this, and we never knew!" Jonah said.

The sight of Jonah, seventy-three years old, pedaling a rusty bicycle over Chinese roads to remote villages, swaying under the load of a forty-pound rucksack was unforgettable.

"It's a miracle you are still fit enough to do this," the missionary said jokingly.

"That's exactly what it is," he replied, seriously. "It is at times like this that I feel the strength of the Lord. It is hard to be constantly available when you are extremely tired. Of course, it does help that the road here is flat!" he said with a big laugh as he pedaled on into the night.

Looking Inward: Sometimes it seems we have no strength to go on; the inner well of our soul seems painfully dry, and the burden gets heavier all the time. Then suddenly God breaks through and shows us someone even weaker, someone in deeper need. And from nowhere, as we reach — up to God and outward to others — the water of life seems to flow out of nowhere.

Looking Outward: Seventy-three years old, twenty hours on a train, and five miles on a rickety bicycle because someone needed to hear the gospel. May God give us, as he gave to Brother Jonah, "a back for any bed, a face for any weather, a stomach for any food, and strength for any work."

W.W.
Open Doors

Seventeen

Brother Jonah
And the Party Boss

China

Faith is to believe what you do not yet see: the reward for this faith is to see what you believe. —St. Augustine, *Sermons*

Seventy-three year old Jonah, mentioned earlier, was preparing to leave a prayer meeting for his home in Shanghai. Just as he was leaving the house there was a loud knock on the door—usually not a good sign.

To everyone's horror it was the local communist party boss. "Which of you is the evangelist Jonah?" he asked. By now he was well known by the authorities, and he was considered an "undesirable" in that part of the country.

"I am," the aged evangelist answered, fearing the worst.

"Will you come and pray for my son? He is very sick and the doctor doesn't know what the problem is."

It was the words of the nobleman who came to Jesus in Cana pleading, "Sir, come down before my child dies!" (John 4:49).

"Why have you come to me? What makes you think I can help?" Jonah asked the party boss.

"Because I heard you are in touch with a God of real power," he answered.

Jonah persisted, "Why do you think I should be willing to ask God to heal your son? After all, you have not shown much liking for Christians yourself."

Tension mounted in the room. Some thought Jonah had gone too far, but that was because they didn't yet understand the spiritual wisdom of this old man.

56

The party boss had a lot of power. He could have had Jonah thrown in jail. But the depth of the man's need showed in his face. Like the nobleman who reached out to Jesus, his only concern was for the healing of his son.

"I have also heard that Christians are full of love," he pleaded, "and that they forgive their enemies."

Jonah pressed on. "Do you think that is true?" he asked. "What possible sense does it make to reach out in love to enemies?"

Speaking with deep emotion the party boss broke down. "All my life I have been taught to hate—to hate tradition, capitalism, to hate the West, to hate the revisionists. Always the cry is 'hate, hate, hate.' And I know I have accomplished nothing, and China has gone nowhere. I know that hate only kills. My wife is dead, my family is dead, and sometimes I feel dead myself. Hatred killed all of them, and it is killing me. But I still feel love, love for my son. I know that without that little love I bear for him, and he for me, I am dead. Maybe your God will take pity on my sick son."

There was a deathly silence around the room, for no one had ever heard a party man speak so frankly about his feelings before.

Then the wisdom of Jonah began to be understood. "We do worship a God of love, and He is the One who has given you the love you have for your son. But you don't have to ask me to pray for your son. Why not speak to God yourself about him?"

So that was where Jonah was leading the man.

"Now you pray, and we will pray with you," Jonah said.

Haltingly, the distraught father put together a fragment of pure, simple prayer: "God, since you are love, save my son, and free him to live a life of love."

We all chanted "Amen," and hurried after him to see his son.

Jesus had told the nobleman, who came to Cana, "Go your way; your son lives" (John 4:50). And the God of love who raised up the nobleman's son touched the son of the party boss that day.

When Jonah finally boarded his train for Shanghai that day, he left two more believers behind, united in love to the Lord Jesus Christ. John recorded, of that earlier event, "And he himself believed, and his whole household" (John 4:53).

Looking Inward: A hostile world is filled with people who often shun us because of our faith, even ridicule us at times for our "narrowness." In our hearts, we are tempted to anger and bitterness toward our tormentors. In times like that we need to remember that until we allow God to pour His love into us, His love can't flow out of us.

Looking Outward: The party boss, in his deep anxiety, could think of nothing but how to get help for his dying son. A wiser soul, Jonah, looked beyond the child's illness to two souls who were spiritually dead. May we, like Jonah, in ministering to the physical and emotional pain of others, never lose sight of the person's deeper need for a right relationship to Jesus Christ.

W.W.
Open Doors

Eighteen

Can That Be
The Same Joseph?

Kenya

We are members of that body which was nailed to the cross,
laid in a tomb, and raised to life on the third day. There is only
one organism of the new creation, and we are members of that
organism, which is Christ. —Lionel Thornton, *The Common
Life of the Body of Christ*

In a crowded ward of Tenwek Hospital in Kenya, a thin old
man dangled his feet over the side of his bed. The patient's eyes
were fixed on the smiling, dark-eyed man in brown pants, carrying
a large Bible, who had just walked through the door. Bed by bed,
he was coming down the aisle between the long rows of hospital
beds. The new arrival was the new hospital chaplain, Joseph. He
had a big smile for every patient.

The old man looked troubled, as if he saw something familiar
about the smiling chaplain. The old fellow had many things to be
troubled about.

One night many months before he and his friends had severely
beaten and left for dead a man named Joseph. This man with the
big smile looked very much like him. But it couldn't be the same
man.

The old man stared for a while—then turned away, as if a pang
of remorse had struck him. Glancing around, he appeared to be
trying to dismiss some dark memory.

He had often wondered what had happened to that one he
and his friends had beaten so badly. Someone said some of the

village people had taken pity on him and brought him to the hospital.

No one could have blamed them, knowing as everyone did all the trouble Joseph had brought to the people of the village. *Even if that scoundrel had died that night, he deserved it,* he once thought, remembering how Joseph grabbed and stole anything and everything he could from anyone he could—borrowing money and never repaying. He would offer to run errands for people, take their money and run away with it. *He deserved every blow that fell on him that night!* the old man had once said.

The smiling figure moved down the aisle, talking first to this patient and then another. Occasionally he would open up his large Bible and read a few verses, pray with a patient, and move on down between the rows of hospital beds.

Finally the chaplain was standing in front of the old man, shining a warm, disarming smile at him, love seeming to radiate from his dark eyes.

The patient decided to start the conversation. "What ever happened to your brother?" he asked gruffly.

"What brother?" Joseph asked.

"You know," the frail man replied. "The one named Joseph who was the talk of the whole village. No one could trust him—the one who stole from everyone and lied all the time."

The chaplain stood quietly for a few minutes, looking deeply into the patient's eyes, as if a glint of recognition had broken through. His face brightened, and his smile widened into a laugh. Then he spoke, "My friend, that was not my brother. I was that person. I am Joseph!"

Stunned to silence, the old man's mouth dropped open as he shrunk back from the smiling chaplain. Before he could say anything, Joseph spoke again.

"Yes, I'm Joseph. But not the same man you knew years ago."

He went on to explain what had happened to him as he had lain on one of these same beds and heard another chaplain explain to him how a sinful man could be made over again, how he could be born again by trusting in Jesus Christ.

After Joseph had recovered from his beating, he returned to the hospital, brimming over with new life. Filled with gratitude, he asked what he could do to help. It was decided that after some training, he could serve on the hospital wards as a chaplain.

"You see," Joseph said to the man on the bed, "you did not recognize me because I am a different man now. I am changed because of what God has done for me."

Joseph opened his Bible, and read, "Therefore, if anyone is in Christ, he is a new creation; old things have passed away; behold, all things have become new" (2 Corinthians 5:17).

It was one thing to walk through the hospital ward, read the Scriptures, and pray with patients. It was a another thing to become that sermon. The message of new life being preached was being lived out before their eyes.

Looking Inward: The Spirit of God moves within, drawing, wooing, urging us to turn loose and allow a new vitality to take over. We struggle and fail, and then we understand that this quickening within is the life of Jesus Christ Himself. Once we surrender control to Him, a fountain of new life, strength, power, and love comes sparkling forth.

Looking Outward: Covered lamps soon grow dark. Cool water, not offered to thirsty people quickly becomes tepid. New life within wants to become new life lived out before others. People search in vain for Truth about God that He intended us to teach by demonstration.

W.W.
World Gospel Mission (WGM)

Nineteen

Lallani
A Precious Gift

Sri Lanka

> Not what we give, but what we share,
> For the gift without the giver is bare.
> Who gives of himself with his alms feeds three,
> Himself, his hungry neighbor, and Me. —J.R. Lowell

Deo and Elaine Miller twelve years ago began Heart of Compassion, a ministry on the island nation of Sri Lanka. Of all the children their ministry has touched, Lallani reached the deepest into their hearts.

Lallani is a beautiful girl, thin, with dainty Caucasian features. When they first met her, Lallani parted her long, black hair in the middle and drew it back in a ponytail. Bright, almond-shaped eyes accentuated her oval face and her little pug nose. Her white, ruffled dress with a torn sash was much too short for her. She looked about six years old, but malnutrition had stunted her growth—she was actually nine.

The Millers, on their first trip to Sri Lanka, stayed with Pastor Colton who they had met in America. Lallani lived next door to the pastor. Deo met her one day standing near the pastor's fence. After that they visited every day until one day Lallani asked, "Why don't you come to my home?"

Never having crossed the fence surrounding the pastor's property, Deo wondered what was on the other side. The dense foliage made it impossible to see beyond the barbed wire. He asked, "Where do you live?"

"Come, come see," she invited, shyly taking his hand. Lifting her over the fence, Deo and his wife, Elaine, followed her into a small village just over a hundred yards from the pastor's home.

Sixty or seventy scattered shanties made up the village. Each hut was about ten feet square, no larger than most American kitchens. Some were attached to the huts next door. Others stood alone. Roofs were thatched coconut palm fronds or an occasional piece of sheet metal. Pounded dirt floors, as hard as concrete, were worn smooth by many bare feet.

An occasional tree, with its trunk looking sandpapered smooth, provided little shade from the sweltering sun. Bark had been stripped off long ago for cooking fires. Children, garbed in rags, ran to gain a closer look at the tall foreign visitor. Lallani gripped Deo's hand. She told her friends in Sinhala, "This is my friend, Uncle Deo." Sinhalese use the term "uncle" and "aunt" to refer to any older person as terms of endearment.

To Deo's surprise, no cooking fires burned in the entire village. Without refrigeration or electricity in such dwellings, food normally simmered constantly on open fires in all villages—but not here.

Men stood in the doorways asking with their eyes, *Who is this stranger who has come to our village?* Many adults sat idly. Since it was three o'clock in the afternoon, Deo asked Lallani, "Why aren't they working? Why don't I smell food cooking?"

She answered, "No work this season. Not eating," was the little girl's reply.

"Wait a minute," he gasped. "What do you mean, `not eating?'"

Lallani's eyes sadly stared at the ground. "No food to eat. Come and sit."

Although he had never entered one of the huts before, he accepted her gracious invitation and followed Lallani through the opening. Everything the family owned could be seen from the doorway. Small straw mats used for sleeping were rolled up in a corner. Black mud walls rose to a height of about six feet. A few pieces of clothing hung on a nail protruding from the wall. The dirt floor had been swept clean, but the musty odor of previous cooking fires hung in the air. The sparsely thatched roof gave little protection from the sun and even less from the torrential rains common to that area. A single kerosene oil lamp belched black smoke, mixing with the odors of damp earth and warm bodies.

Deo became uncomfortable, realizing that these people lived in this situation perpetually. The sight was too much for him. He felt like an intruder in spite of their hospitality. Something had to be done, and now.

Deo and Elaine left the village and headed for nearby shops to buy food for the villagers. With Lallani's suggestions, they bought rice, a large fish, vegetables, fruit—even a cake when they saw Lallani's mouth watering at the sight of it. Back in the village, they decided to have a feast, and numerous people began cooking the bounty. Lallani ran through the village inviting all her relatives and special friends to the feast. It was a day the villagers never forgot.

After that Lallani waited in Colton's yard by the fence for Deo every afternoon. She often took his hand, and they returned to her village. He may have been the first white man to visit her family and friends. He often read them Bible stories and taught them about Jesus.

The day arrived when it was time to say goodbye; the Millers "vacation" in Sri Lanka was at an end. The last morning, Deo walked out on the veranda. He was surprised to see Lallani standing there. Normally she left early, because she walked for an hour to reach the school.

He waved to her, and she ran over to him. "Why aren't you in school?" he asked.

Looking at the ground, she replied, "Uncle, I took leave from school today."

"Lallani! I told you how important it is not to miss a day of school. Even though Mommy and Daddy might not force you to go to school, you must attend every day. You have to get an education." Education would be the only way she could ever break the vicious cycle of poverty.

She could tell he was upset with her. Shyly, she continued, "I'm staying home because you are going back to America. I'll never see you again. I must stay with you to the end."

Deo stepped toward her and placed his hands on her shoulders. At a loss for words, he wanted to give her one more thing, but all his trinkets, candy, and gum were gone.

Then he reached in his shirt pocket and pulled out his worn New Testament that he always carried. Over the years, he had underlined it and written in the margins. The pages were crinkled and bent. "Lallani, I want to leave this valuable book with you. Don't let your parents sell it. It tells stories about Jesus."

Lallani nodded her head. Her lower lip quivered.

He swallowed and said, "I will pray for you, Lallani, and for your parents, too." A lump formed in his throat. He could not speak. He felt as if he was deserting his own child.

Lallani cried softly. "Never see you again, Uncle."

He put his arms around this special little girl and held her for a moment.

"No, no. You can't leave yet. Mommy is making toffee," she exclaimed.

Deo thought she said "coffee," and replied, "We don't have time to drink coffee, because the plane won't wait for us. I have to leave now, honey. I'm sorry."

Again Lallani pleaded, "You must wait. Mommy is making toffee."

"We have to leave now. I will pray for you daily, Lallani." Deo whispered, barely able to speak. Quickly he turned and walked back from the edge of the jungle not daring to look back. Once seated in the Volkswagen, he leaned out the window and waved to the little girl who meant so much to him.

He couldn't get Lallani out of his mind as they drove away from Colton's house. What if she died? Did she understand about Jesus? He felt utterly helpless. Yet, he could do no more at this point.

Arriving at the church, they transferred the luggage to a van. Suddenly, a runner raced up with a crinkled piece of paper. "Sir, Sir, this is for you!" he shouted breathlessly.

A string wrapped around the gift held a small tag that read: To Uncle Deo and Aunt Elaine. Deo unwrapped the package and found small, brown cubes inside that smelled like ginger and brown sugar. Several people gathered around to see what the present was. "It must be a sweet of some kind," he said.

The pastor's wife took a piece and ate it. She exclaimed. "Ah, this is homemade toffee. Where did you get it?"

Elaine answered, "Lallani's mother must have made it for us."

Each ate a square of the delicious candy. The pastor looked serious. "You don't understand what this gift really means, do you?"

"It was thoughtful of them to make us a going away present," Deo replied.

"No, no. You don't understand what a precious gift you are holding in your hand!" exclaimed Colton. "Sugar is the highest priced commodity in Sri Lanka. Your friends must have gathered all the rupees in the village to buy the ingredients for that toffee! The entire village won't eat for several days. That is their way of showing how much they love and appreciate you. They must have given you all they had."

Looking Inward: In the back of the Miller's freezer, a crinkled piece of paper holds three small cubes of brown sugar and ginger. Some days when Deo needs encouragement, he takes out the little package to glimpse the meaning of love and sacrifice. Over the years many have held in their hands the toffee Lallani's mother made. Sacrificial gifts are always, as the Apostle Paul said, "a sweet-smelling aroma, an acceptable sacrifice, well pleasing to God" (Philippiansd 4:18).

Looking Outward: Deo returned home asking himself, What am I willing to give in return? Two years later it became apparent, as he and Elaine returned to set up the Heart of Compassion, a ministry feeding and vocationally training thousands of children in Sri Lanka. Sri Lankan nationals staff the centers and provide the gospel to these young, eager minds. Lallani is now twenty-one, still carrying her little Testament given her many years ago.

S.T.O.
Heart of Compassion
Story adapted from *You Start with One,* Deo Miller with Susan F. Titus, published by Thomas Nelson Pub., 1990.

Twenty

Fred Magbauna
The Voice of God Speaks

Philippines

Faith isn't really faith until it is all that you are holding on to. —Tim Hansel

---

A bright midnight moon swept white light over the transmitter buildings of Christian Radio City Manila. It picked out the figure of a guard as he passed between inky pools of tree shade, his torch darting in the blackness like stabs of summer lightning.

Inside the building, colored monitor lights flickered on an array of electronic equipment. Technicians worked late into the night on a new transmitter.

Night sounds carried across the heavy atmosphere with astounding clarity. The footsteps of an announcer crunched on the gravel as he walked along the roadway between the hushed compound houses. The muffled sounds of gospel broadcasting in unfamiliar tongues filtered into the night air. The operator checked the overseas schedules to make certain the message of Jesus Christ kept rendezvous with listeners near and far.

A tall antenna tower, pinnacled by red warning lights, stood sentinel over the night-hushed scene. But something on the tower was terribly wrong. At the top a man, held by his head, dangled helplessly three hundred feet above the ground!

Fred Magbauna, Director of Far East Broadcasting Company, Philippines, later described that awful moment:

"The program I had just recorded was a message on Romans 12:1-2. It was almost time for it to be aired. I had dropped off the recorded program with the operator. As I was leaving the compound, I noticed the burned-out warning light on the top of the antenna. This was dangerous, since low-flying aircraft might fly into it. The lamp had to be changed. I threw the ground switch, not realizing the high voltage wasn't effectively grounded. Then I climbed the three-hundred-foot tower." At the top of the tower he felt a jolt.

"Suddenly, ten thousand watts of radio frequency current was burning me alive! My head felt like it was locked in a vice held precariously in an electromagnetic field.

Is this death? I wondered. Then, through the sparking and arcing, I heard my own voice saying, `I beseech you therefore, brethren, by the mercies of God, that you present your bodies a living sacrifice . . .' I realized that my own program was going out over the antenna, and my head, locked by the radio frequency power, was acting as a conductor. As I lost consciousness, I cried, `Lord, I commend to you my spirit.' Then I fell.

"I regained consciousness a few moments later eight feet below. My leg was caught on a brace, which saved me from a deadly fall to the ground. A fuse blew, causing my release. A few seconds more, and I would have burned to death."

Still on the ladder, Fred thought of the decision that had faced him and the unanswered letter he had received from an old classmate from the U.S. His friend was urging him to accept an engineering job with high starting pay.

He read the letter to his wife, Aliw, who was not impressed. "I don't care how good the salary is," she said. "You made a promise to the Lord never to take a job that was not connected with spreading the gospel."

"We could support pastors with that extra money," Fred explained. But Aliw would not agree. That night when Fred went to the station to record his program, he decided to write an acceptance for the job anyway and tell his wife later.

Fred had grown up in Negros Province in a traditional Philippine religion. As a young boy during World War II, he saw bombs, fear, and death everywhere. Then shortly after the war ended, he heard the gospel preached over FEBC stations and received Christ as his Savior. He had wanted to go to Bible school, but his family needed his financial help. Instead, he studied to be a civil engineer, but determined to serve his Lord however possible. He joined a team that went from village to village, preaching the gospel. It was then that he met Aliw, the girl he eventually married before he began working for FEBC as an engineer and broadcaster.

Hanging on the transmitter tower that night, the words of his own message touched him.

"Fred," God seemed to say, "You were telling others to surrender their lives to Me, but you yourself were trying to run away to New York to better yourself."

Dazed and seriously injured, Fred miraculously descended the open ladder alone, fearing each step would be his last. God kept him conscious till he reached the ground and somehow staggered to the compound nurse's home. He was rushed to the hospital in almost unbearable pain, his head severely burned. A dozen deep holes, the largest four inches in diameter, had burned like charcoal clear to the skull. With hundreds of Christians praying for him, and after three months in the hospital, the X-rays showed no brain damage. The healing was complete.

During his recovery, Fred had plenty of time to think. Temptation came, as it frequently does, but Fred said of that night he hung from the tower: "It is a fearful thing to fall into the hands of the Living God!"

On the hospital bed, Fred renewed his promise to God never to take a job that was not connected with spreading the gospel. With a staff of more than two hundred, Fred Magbanua became Managing Director, responsible for twenty-one domestic and overseas broadcasting stations in the Philippines that broadcast the Good News of Jesus Christ in seventy-one languages and dialects all across Asia.

Looking Inward: Temptation comes to each of us in many different ways. Sometimes we are tempted to compromise our values or to place too much emphasis on material things. Sometimes, like Fred, we are tempted to accept jobs and to go places that are not in God's will for us. How important it is for us to be in tune with God's plan for our lives.

Looking Outward: What a significant part this humble man of God has played in the growth of Far East Broadcasting Company. He directed an operation that beams the gospel to two-thirds of the world's population. Through a dramatic incident in his life, Fred became aware of what God desired him to do. How different his life might have been if he had followed his own desires. Seeking guidance from the Lord is imperative in planning our futures.

S.T.O.
Far East Broadcasting Company (FEBC)
Story adapted from *Eyes Beyond the Horizon,* by Eleanor G. Bowman with Susan F. Titus, published by Thomas Nelson, 1991.

Twenty-one

Makwingi
The Fish Story

Zaire

The smallest link in the chain of God's great purpose is worth your service. —Vance Havner

---

Arriving in Knungu, the government headquarters for that area of Zaire, Abe Kroeger entered the office of the Belgian administrator to take care of some of business with the government. The administrator, although not a believer, had always been friendly and expressed interest in the missionary work through Bible Literature Fellowship that Abe and Mary were doing in the village of Matende, several miles outside Knungu.

"How are things going there at your mission?" the administrator asked as Abe sat down.

"Rather slowly," Abe said, almost complaining.

The administrator answered with words Abe never forgot: "*Ce n'est pas la quantity qui compte, mais la quality*," he said, with a big smile." (It's not the quantity that counts, but the quality.)

Abe was stunned to silence. "Yes," he said, "you are right."

On the drive back to the mission, Abe felt a little ashamed, even though he still felt his answer, "Rather slowly" had been correct.

What made both Abe's and the administrator comment correct was a young boy named Makwingi. Several months before he had come to Abe and Mary asking for baptism. He had been listening for a long time to the Bible stories Mary had been teaching to young boys and girls who came to the mission.

He came with many questions: "Was the God the white men talked about the only true God? Could He *really* take away sin and make a person clean inside?"

Abe and Mary had questions, too. Was this young boy who spent his days catching rats, grasshoppers, or an occasional bird to eat, really serious about wanting to be baptized? Food was scarce, so Makwingi and his friends would do anything for food. He could barely read, and he had been taught so little about the Bible. How could he be certain?

Makwingi explained again that he was certain, that he now believed in Jesus, and that he wanted to be baptized as soon as possible.

"I wasn't sure before," he explained, "but I decided the other day when I was fishing. We needed some food, so I wanted very much to catch some fish that day for my family. You remember that story you told about the man named Peter, who was fishing in his boat and how Jesus had helped him to catch many fish," he explained. "Well, that day, in my boat I said that I would find out for sure if God was real and if he would help me. I said to God, `If I catch a fish today, I will believe in You.'"

"What happened?" Abe asked him.

"I caught many fish that day," he said smiling. "So when I got back, I bowed to the ground and told Jesus that I now believed in Him as the only true God who could save me from sin."

For days Abe and Mary wondered about the "fish story." But day after day, the unswerving faith of Makwingi, the only believer in his family, convinced them that the God who told Peter, "Put out the nets for a catch" had also spoken to their little friend Makwingi.

"Sometimes God's miracles come in small packages," Abe said later. And now, on his way home from Knungu, the administrator's words came back to him: *"Ce n'est pas la quantity qui compte, mais la quality."* Abe knew in his heart that the man was right.

Looking Inward: We chide ourselves for the big tasks left undone. And we should keep our hearts set on them; but sometimes the little things left undone bother us very little or not at all. Often it is these little things that prove to be the unpolished gems that enrich our souls.

Looking Outward: Expectations of others, and the spiritual growth we want to see there, often run so high that we slink away in defeat and discouragement when nothing seems to be happening. We fail sometimes to see the tiny grains of sand God is washing up on the shores of another's life that areslowly but steadily building a beautiful and wide clean white sandy beach.

W.W.
Bible Literature Fellowship (BLF)

Twenty-two

Matthew's Walk with God

Chad

If faith can see every step of the way, it is not faith. — William Barclay

---

Matthew and Larry sat eyeball to eyeball. Absent were the former pleasantries that accompanied previous appeals. Defiance hung heavy in the air.

Matthew was President of the student body of the Evangelical Bible Institute (EBI) in Moundou, Chad, Africa. Behind him sat members of the student executive committee. They demanded, for the third time, an additional twenty-five dollar a month living allowance.

Although Larry Gray was Director of the Institute, he couldn't grant their request. The school board had ruled out a financial increase.

EBI provided its students a living allowance of thirty-eight dollars a month. From that they paid for rent, utilities, food, toiletries, and medicine. Their home churches tried to help with food by sending sacks of grain, but often they were unable. Sometimes they forgot. Many students were married and had children. Unlike some other countries, part-time jobs were not available.

So with grain sacks near empty in late October and the living allowance not due for several more days, the atmosphere was tense. The students threatened to strike unless they received more money.

As Larry stared at Matthew, his emotions fluctuated between abject fear and white-hot anger. *Oh, great! Two months as director and the whole school's ready to fall apart,* he thought. A minute later, *Who do they think they are? They get a full academic scholarship and a living allowance. They don't know how good they have it.*

In the midst of these thoughts, Larry took time to seek wisdom from God. After a brief silent prayer, he assured Matthew and the others that he recognized their dilemma. He shared from his own experience in college and seminary of God's amazing provision when human resources were exhausted.

The students did not look convinced. Larry asked them to pray with him. His words met with silence.

So he prayed alone. With the strike imminent, Larry steeled himself to first expel the instigator, Matthew. But before the decision was made, something totally unforeseen happened. From an unexpected source, enough food arrived to feed them for the rest of the month.

That day in chapel, a totally new atmosphere prevailed. The students sang praises to the Lord with hearts overflowing. A miracle began to unfold.

November, December, January, and February, when they found themselves in that "empty sack" fourth week, they united to call on their Heavenly Father for daily bread. Attitudes changed. Motivation was strengthened, momentum surged, and grade point averages rose. A spirit of family unity pervaded the campus. Matthew even invited Larry to his house for a big feast. There he confided, "Mr. Larry has taught us to walk with God." Larry felt a lump form in his throat because, more than anything else, he wanted God to be real to his students. Matthew, a natural-born leader, would help set the course for the rest of them.

Then in February, heat and sickness struck the campus with vengeance bringing malaria, dysentery, and hepatitis. Students and their children were laid low. Class attendance was halved, and three students were hospitalized.

Larry turned again to God, who had answered their prayers the previous five months. He was certain God would see them through this time.

One by one the ill ones gradually recovered. Everyone returned to class—all but one. Matthew was still battling a strong case of hepatitis. Slowly he gained strength and returned home after three weeks in the hospital, still very weak.

As Larry sat by his student's bed, Matthew fretted about how far behind he was in his courses. "Mr. Larry," he asked, "do you think I'll still be able to graduate in May?"

"Matthew," Larry replied, keeping a light tone to his voice, "We'll graduate you even if we have to turn this bedroom into a classroom."

Twelve hours later, Matthew suffered a relapse. Larry rushed him, semi-comatose, to TEAM's medical center in Bebalem, an hour and a half away. There, in intensive care, he fought death day and night, but he was not alone. Classes were suspended. Everyone prayed like they had never prayed before.

As Larry knelt by Matthew's bed, he pleaded fervently with God for this special student's life. But on Friday, February 23, 1990, Matthew Bamaskine, student president, former adversary, and well-won friend, went to be with the Lord three months before graduation. He was thirty-one years old and left behind a wife of ten years, Rachel, and four children, all under seven years old.

Matthew had reached the highest level of biblical training of any of the students. He would have been the most likely candidate to translate the Bible into the Gabri language. There was no one on the immediate horizon to replace him.

Larry preached the memorial service although it was difficult for him. The rest of his classmates graduated and are now ministering, many of them still praying that they may fill the shoes of Matthew as a spiritual helper for the Gabri people.

Looking Inward: When God's answer is sometimes "No," we don't always understand why. But He never promised to give us all "yes" answers. God promised to give us Himself, and He is enough.

Looking Outward: More than anything else, we want God to be real to those we minister to. Our actions, our words, and our faith are the ingredients that make this happen. Our goal should be to have someone say of us as Matthew did when he said, "Mr. Larry has taught us to walk with God."

S.T.O.
Evangelical Bible Institute (TEAM)

Twenty-three

Berta
Looking for Milk

Nicaragua

I wanted to go, He said stay.
I wanted to do, He said pray;
I wanted to work, He said wait,
I wanted to live for His sake!
"Love Me, child," He softly said,
"Oh, yes, Lord," I bowed my head;
"I want your way, I am your son,
Not my will, but Thine be done!" —Grace Opperman

Today was a sad day for Berta. For years she had attended the Bible classes offered by CAM International in Managua. She was able to attend the first two sessions of a new course on Saturday and Sunday. But over the weekend, the Sandanistas had called for a week-long strike.

Everything was in disarray. Paving stones had been torn from the streets to form barricades. She had counted on the Bible course to help her work with the women and children who came weekly to her house for Bible study. She always looked forward to the classes, and she was deeply disappointed when she learned that the buses wouldn't be running.

Alone at home, she began to cry out to God. "Why, if I am studying Your Word do you allow this to happen?" she asked. For several hours she kept up her prayers, pouring out her disappointment to the Lord as she went about her work.

Later that morning, she stopped her prayers when she heard a noise at the front of her house. Looking up, she saw eight women standing at her door.

"We are wondering if you know where we might buy cow's milk," one of them asked. The trouble in town had thrown these women in disarray also. Evidently they had been searching all around and decided to go together in their search.

"Why, yes!" Berta answered. "My son's wife sells milk. She hasn't arrived yet, but she should be coming here soon." Berta invited them to come inside to wait.

Time passed, but Berta's daughter-in-law still hadn't arrived. The women began to grow restless and started to complain, first about one thing and then another. Soon they were talking about how terrible the situation in Nicaragua was becoming.

Berta decided she must do something. Getting out her Bible, she began talking to them about God, about how He loved everyone, and how His Son had died for a sinning world. Beginning with Adam and Eve, she explained that everyone had sinned and needed to come to the Savior.

These were women who had never heard the gospel, and now in Berta's living room they were hearing it for the first time. They had come for cow's milk. Berta smiled to herself as she realized she had this opportunity to dispense another kind of milk, the kind the Apostle Peter spoke about: "As newborn babes, desire the pure milk of the word, that you may grow thereby" (1 Peter 2:2).

On and on the Bible lesson went. Berta's daughter-in-law, her travel plans also upset by the trouble in town, never did arrive with the milk. But the women didn't seem to complain, for Berta's milk was feeding their hungry souls.

The strike continued for several days. Since the women couldn't go to work, they decided to come back to Berta's house for the next two days. On Thursday only three of them could return, but each of them prayed that morning to receive Christ as her Savior.

Berta then thought about her prayer of disappointment that Monday morning. It soon became clear to her why He hadn't allowed her to go to the Bible class. Because the buses weren't running that Monday, these three women, all of whom started coming every Tuesday for the women's Bible class, found nourishment beyond what they sought. And Berta had the joy of sharing it with them.

Looking Inward: Angry at disappointments, we may miss a more important divine appointment. God knows what He is doing in our souls, even when it seems things are going wrong.

Looking Outward: The world is filled with people whose spirits are starving for the bread of life. Many of them feel the ravages of their hunger, but few understand what it takes to satisfy it. Jesus, the Bread of Life who came down to feed the spiritually hungry, said "Simon, son of Jonah, do you love Me? . . . Feed My Sheep" (John 21:17).

W.W.
CAM International

Twenty-four

How Big Are Miracles?

Niger Republic

The "wages" of every noble work do yet lie in Heaven or else nowhere. —Thomas Carlyle, *Past and Present*

It was a trip I would have avoided if I could. The balky old Jeep pickup truck was becoming more undependable by the day. Heavy rains had wiped out most of the roads there on the southern border of the Niger Republic. Even so, I had no choice but to make the journey. A sick man's life depended on it. He had a high fever and was not responding to the anti-malarial medication. We had done all we could for him at the small SIM International facility. His only hope was to get to a hospital more than a hundred miles away.

Our medical dispenser came along to help me. He sat in the bed of the pickup truck, cradling the patient in his arms to protect him from the worst bumps in the road. I prayed with every mile that the vehicle would hold up long enough for us to reach the government hospital in Zinder, on the southern rim of the Sahara Desert.

The rainfall north of us had been heavier than I had expected. Dry desert sands quickly turned to a quagmire during the short but heavy rainy season. The roadbed we followed totally disappeared in spots.

Coming around a bend in the road, I saw what I feared most. In a low spot in the road, the rainwater runoff had totally filled the valley through which the road passed. Ahead lay a small lake, perhaps two hundred or more yards across. I remembered that the roadbed was built up a bit to accommodate the rainy season. I also remembered that the high one-lane roadbed created a six or eight-foot drop-off on either side of the road.

I braked the truck and tried to determine where the road ran and how high above the road surface the water had risen. There was no way to tell.

I looked back at the dispenser. The despair on his face mirrored my own. The brush was so thick and the terrain so rough on either side of the water, we could never drive around it to the other side. The road had been our only hope, and now that looked closed.

The sick man, lying on his mat in the back of the truck, now seemed weaker, and his breathing was becoming more labored. And we were still more than forty miles from the hospital in Zinder.

Where was God? Or where was Moses' rod to strike the waters and part the sea in front of us? Had God mocked us, bringing us this far, only to have to turn back and perhaps take a dead man home to his village?

It didn't seem fair. My prayers at that moment were more a complaint than a claim of victory. I rested my head on my arms, folded over the steering wheel, exhausted from having fought the vehicle for more than four hours over the marshy terrain.

In a few moments two African men happened along. At first they gave me only grunts for a greeting. My white skin still set me apart, made me a stranger, and an unwanted one at that.

But then they came abreast of the truck. First one, then the other stopped and gazed at the sick man. They mumbled something to the dispenser, who explained where we were going and why.

The men looked at me again. In a split-second they seemed to reinterpret the situation. Their expressions changed. I was no longer one of the white men who had come to profit or take advantage of them. I was someone who cared enough for one of their own kind to risk a journey over difficult terrain at the worst possible time of year.

Then a strange thing happened. What I remember most was the whiteness of one man's long flowing robe. Carefully he gathered up the folds of cloth and held them tightly around his waist with one hand. Slipping off his rawhide sandals, he looped them together and dangled them around his neck. Then he waded out into the water, feeling along the edge of the roadbed with his bare feet and the long walking stick the men often carried on long walks. He motioned for me to follow in the truck.

Carefully, I started the engine and inched the Jeep into the waters, making sure I wasn't going in so deep that the engine would stall. That would certainly end the trip! With each step, as he plumbed the edges of the roadbed, he looked back and urged me on.

Step by step, he pointed to the water level on his bare legs, showing me the depth of the water. It took about fifteen minutes for him to track out the roadbed and lead me to the other side.

Twenty more feet—then ten, then the tires swished in the soft mud on the other side. He turned and smiled broadly, as if to say, "We did it!"

With deep feelings welling up in me and my eyes becoming watery, I could hardly see to steer. He hadn't asked for money or anything else. In fact, I had never thought of the solution he offered. He just waded out, this dark-skinned Moses with his long stick, parting the waters for me to pass through on safe ground.

I offered to pay him, but he refused. Still smiling, perhaps at his own deed well done, he waved us a final goodbye and turned to go. I watched through the rear view mirror as he retraced his steps back through the water to his friend waiting for him on the other side.

How big is a miracle—how spectacular does something have to be to qualify for a supernatural happening? True, God could have just made the waters roll back so I could see the hidden roadbed. But we didn't really need to see waters roll back—we just needed to get to the other side. And the "Moses" God sent along that day had accomplished that feat just as well.

I will never know if my kind helper that day was a believer, whether he had been disposed to help me because he loved God and wanted to serve Him, as I did. He could have been among the thousands who heard the gospel message on one of the many tiny transistor radios scattered all over the desert and responded to what light he had received. Or perhaps he did it because I was helping "one of his own." And perhaps the sick man, who made it to the hospital that day and lived through his ordeal, may never understand the part this stranger played in his rescue.

For that matter, I won't know until eternity if it was a human or an angel, sent from heaven to minister to saints in need.

Of one thing I am sure. I drove away from that flood pond more certain than ever that God reaches out to us when we need Him most and when we're reaching out to those who need us.

"'When did we see You sick . . . and come to You?' And the King will answer and say to them, 'Assuredly, I say to you, inasmuch as you did it to one of the least of these My brethren, you did it to Me.'" (Matthew 25:39-40).

Looking Inward: One of the greatest sins I can commit today is to see myself as the center of the universe. When I do, I blind myself to what God might want to achieve in me. Yet, if I keep my eyes focused on Him, He can accomplish His work through me.

Looking Outward: It is no accident that I am here today, doing what I do, seeing the people I see. If I look closely, I'll be able to see with His eyes and reach out with His hands to someone in need.

W.W.
SIM International

<h2>Twenty-five</h2>

The Monk
at St. Sergius Monastery

Russia

Christianity isn't a religion—it's a Man. Knowing this Person is how we obtain salvation. —Author unknown

---

The American tour group was walking the halls of the cathedral, palace, and buildings of the Trinity Monastery of St. Sergius. The monastery is near the city of Zagorsk, about seventy kilometers northeast of Moscow. It was the fall of 1989, during the early days of so-called Glasnost, the more relaxed state of affairs between Russia and Western countries.

The group was awed by the antiquity of the monastery, the lavish expressions of devotion to God that had survived the great Russian Revolution. In 1920, rather than destroy the beautiful edifice, Lenin had proclaimed the Trinity Monastery of St. Sergius to be a state museum of history and art. Today, Russians are allowed to proudly display the church and buildings there as unexcelled examples of medieval art, culture, and architecture.

The tour was being conducted by a black-robed monk from the monastery. In the course of the tour, the monk discovered a familiar voice among the group. At the moment of recognition, the monk's expression softened. He realized that the American standing beside him was Jack Koziol, the broadcaster from Far Eastern Broadcasting Company he had listened to for more than twenty years.

Until then the monk's dark eyes had been remote and expressionless while he conducted the tour. But now his voice took on a different tone. The words of the neatly bearded monk stunned his listeners. "During our times of difficulty, the monks here received great blessing through *Radio Peradache*. I want to thank you on behalf of us all," said the monk as he stood in the courtyard silhouetted by ornate towers and golden onion-shaped domes.

He explained how the monks of St. Sergius had became curators and guides, living without their Holy Scriptures, forbidden to conduct Mass. Their contact with true worship became *Radio Peradache*, FEBC's broadcasts beamed into the Soviet Union.

Although 700,000 visitors toured these historic buildings annually, the monk said he never expected to meet the beloved announcer he listened to in the privacy of his own room, nor had he ever expected to see Bob Bowman, the President of FEBC, also with the tour group that day.

The monk's response was like many others heard about during the group's tour. During the two-week tour, Koziol was asked to preach in his native Russian language, to a number of churches in Minsk, Brest, and Moscow. When Jack's name was announced, a low murmur spread through the congregation. The Russian believers strained to look at the man they had listened to for over thirty years. Now and then the sound of sobbing could be heard as people held handkerchiefs to their eyes and wiped away tears. Whenever the question was asked, "How many listen to *Radio Peradache*?" practically every hand in the audience was raised.

During the closed years it is believed that some 39,750 groups in Russia met around these Christian radio broadcasts, radio churches, as they were called. An estimated 1.59 million became believers through the twenty-two hours of broadcast each day to Russia from transmitters in the Philippines, South Korea, Saipan, and San Francisco.

In 1990, FEBC received more than 40,000 letters from people in the Russian provinces. Since the *Glasnost* window opened, FEBC has sent more than a hundred thousand Bibles, New Testaments, Gospels of John, and Bible commentaries through the mail in response to the requests.

One Russian wrote, "I have waited sixty years to hold a Bible in my hands." Such a letter gives great encouragement to those who labored for years to see that the Word of God penetrated the Iron Curtain. As dark as it appeared to those on the outside looking in, it was encouraging to know that, even in the dark monastery halls the black-clad monk walked, light was shining in. As the Apostle Paul wrote many years ago, "For it is the God who commanded light to shine out of darkness who has shone in our hearts to give the light of the knowledge of the glory of God in the face of Jesus Christ" (2 Corinthians 4:6).

Looking Inward: Unlike the monk and the man who waited sixty years for a Bible, we can hold a Bible in our hands daily. In theory, nothing is stopping us. Yet we allow many things to keep us from the Word, what the Psalmist called "a lamp to my feet and a light to my path" (Psalm 119:105).

Looking Outward: Whether we are speaking or writing, we never know exactly how far our words may travel. Like Jack Koziol, we may reach lives half-way around the world. On the other hand, the most important things we say or do may touch those in our own communities, bringing Christ to someone struggling in darkness. Jesus said, "Let your light so shine" (Matthew 5:16).

S.T.O.
Far East Broadcasting Company (FEBC)
Story adapted from *Eyes Beyond the Horizon,* by Eleanor G. Bowman with Susan F. Titus, published by Thomas Nelson Pub., 1991.

Twenty-six

The Old Woman's Morning Song

Korea

Language can easily be a barrier rather than a bridge, whereas in every language the smile, the gentle touch, the embrace are the same—and in every century, too. —Philip Pare, *God Made the Devil*

Dr. Edward L. Hayes was sitting on a rock, reading his Bible and taking advantage of the early morning sun at this beautiful Korean mountain retreat. Suddenly Ed became aware that someone was watching him. Looking up, he saw an old woman, standing on a quaint bridge spanning the boulder-strewn stream below. Their eyes met and Ed felt a fleeting sensation of recognition—something only one close to a friend or family member would know.

A Christian industrialist, Mr. Hwang, had invited Ed to take a break from his heavy teaching and preaching schedule. He arranged for a bus ticket to the mountains near Taegu below Seoul, Korea. The jarring, bouncy ride over narrow dirt roads led Ed through country of indescribable beauty.

Hills that had been ravaged by decades of foreign exploitation and a costly war had now been reforested. The twisting, colorful trunks of a stunted pine had made a fast comeback, each tree like a giant bonsai set among granite outcroppings on steep hillsides.

86

In "The Land of the Morning Sun" mountains figure prominently in spiritual pilgrimages and prayer retreats. In 1950 a number of Koreans experienced a forced pilgrimage from north to south, escaping from the advancing communists. Among the refugees from the north were many believers, whose sturdy faith and selfless love astounded their fellow countrymen.

The Hwangs were part of this exodus. Carrying their little daughter, In Soon, on their backs, they fled, hiding in the forest by day, walking by night. So it wasn't strange that the call had come for Ed to join Mr. Hwang at the mountain retreat.

Ed stared at the new Bible in his hands, a gift from a Korean pastor. One column on each page was in Korean, the other column in English.

He could tell that the eyesight of the woman on the bridge wasn't good, but she spotted the black book in Ed's hands and instantly knew it was a Bible. He responded by greeting her with the only Korean line he knew, a simple greeting. She replied as if he knew her native language well.

Then a strange thing happened. Aware that words could not adequately convey the language of the heart, she began to sing a hymn. Even in Korean, Ed recognized the English tune. Instantly he knew she must be a believer in Christ.

When she finished her stanza of the hymn, he began one of his own, singing the same hymn in English. For several moments their quaint and antiphonal experience filled the corner of the forest with music. They felt God's unique presence and a bonding in faith. They needed no translator or other expression for their own spiritual song.

There in that Korean forest the living truth of Paul's words in Colossians 3:16 came to life: "Let the word of Christ dwell in you richly in all wisdom, teaching and admonishing one another in psalms and hymns and spiritual songs, singing with grace in your hearts to the Lord."

The eyes of the American man and the old Korean woman met once again. The woman beamed a radiant smile as Ed finished singing. Ed sensed her need, and his own, for deeper communion with the Lord and with each other. But all they could do that morning was gesture, point from their hearts to the sky, and sing.

Twenty years have passed since that incident. Today Korea stands as a model of church growth with a heritage of praying Christians.

Ed will always cherish that spring morning in his memory. Ed lived for years at Mt. Hermon in the California redwoods. The freshness of springtime bursts forth with fragrant flowers and scented pine clothing another conference center in heavenly, living color. And each time Ed reads that special Bible with the angular Korean symbols, he is reminded of the Korean woman on the bridge.

"Christian unity and Christian witness were wed that morning. In the frail hymn-singing voice of a Korean woman and a small black book, two cultures met. I never knew the woman's name, nor did I see her again. But for a few minutes of pure delight, two spirits met as one. Kin we were and shall be for eternity. We joined our spirits with the Spirit of God in a bond of love."

Looking Inward: Sometimes when alone, we may sense the bond of love that draws all believers together. Nothing earthly can adequately describe our union in Christ, which transcends culture, boundaries, language, and race. It was enough that Jesus died, and that His death and resurrection unites us with our Father in heaven.

Looking Outward: The prayer of our Lord, "May they all be one," can only be answered by our will to be one with others. Our differences matter little. Our task is to be of the same mind, to dwell together in unity, and to love one another. The bottom line in Christianity is the simple credo: "One Lord, one faith, one baptism; one God and Father of all, who is above all, and through all, and in you all."

S.T.O.
Mount Hermon

Twenty-seven

John: Walking Patiently
Through the Fire

Niger
Republic

Sorrow and silence are strong,
And patience enduring is godlike.
                    Henry Wadsworth Longfellow, *Evangeline*

A loud knock on the door. Who could be coming at such an hour. John, the young African school principal, rose and lit a small kerosene lantern. Pulling on some clothes, he went to the door. He had been on the job less than a year.

At the door was a group of older men, some of the members of the school board. "We would like to see all your financial records and the money box," they demanded.

He went to the place where he kept the money box hidden, took the bookkeeping records from the shelf and handed it to the men. He cleared a place on his small table for them to examine his record keeping.

Clearly, they didn't trust him. Last week it was the way they settled a frivolous complaint by a student. Before that it was the small patch of weeds one of the board members saw in the schoolyard. It was always something.

What are they trying to do? Why don't they trust me? Why this surprise inspection in the middle of the night? Do they think I am too young for the job? Are they angry that the rest of the board has chosen me as principal instead of someone else? All these questions raced through his mind. He noticed that he was trembling all over, in fear and silent rage.

He watched them carefully add up the columns. Then they counted every franc in the money box. He could almost sense their disappointment when the totals added up perfectly. But all the while his stomach was churning.

"It's all right," they said, without a trace of smile or politeness. He ushered them to the door, said good night and returned to his bed, heavy-hearted and filled with worry. He knew it wasn't the end of the matter. They would keep hounding him until they found some tiny infraction they could use to dismiss him or to make him give up in anger.

The students like me, he thought. *And the other teachers seem happy enough. Why can't these men leave me alone?* Where was God in all this? He prayed: "Lord, I try so hard to live for you, but no one notices. You know I have tried to be honest with everyone. Why don't they trust me? Why does it always seem I'm walking through hot coals?" He thought of the verse from the Psalms: They may shoot in secret at the blameless; suddenly they shoot at him and do not fear (64:4).

Another verse from the Psalms came to him: "Who is the man who fears the Lord? Him shall He teach in the way He chooses (25:12). Late that night, he finally drifted off to sleep.

The next day one of the school boys came from the post office, bringing a handful of letters. One envelope addressed to him caught his eye. It was a letter from the mission headquarters that had years ago founded the school where he was teaching. Tearing it open, he read:

Dear John,

The work here has become too much for our present staff. We very much need an energetic young man of good reputation who is very good with bookkeeping to serve as our business manager. The person would be required to handle considerable sums of money and a lot of detail. I have made numerous inquiries, and several people commented that your work and excellent character shown there at the school would make you an excellent choice for the position. Would appreciate it if you would consider coming to talk with us about this matter.

Signed _____ (Mission Official)

Looking Inward: When others doubt us, it is futile to try to defend ourselves. Our confidence rises from the knowledge that God's eye is upon us, and above all else, we "serve the Lord Christ" (Colossians 3:24).

Looking Outward: When we do our work, as Paul commanded, "Heartily, as to the Lord and not to men" (Colossians 3:23), we can count on God to reward us in His way and in His time. Evil people may scorn us, but God loves those who serve Him.

W. W.
SIM International

Twenty-eight

Penninah
Buried Alive

India

Only love enables humanity to grow, because love engenders life and it is the only form of energy that lasts forever. — Michel Quoist, *With Open Heart*

Penninah smiled lovingly at the beautiful child on her lap, her newborn son. How different a scene it was from the story she had been telling throughout the Mukti villages of India, where she had shared a story of love with people of her tribe.

Two years before, Penninah had married a fine young Indian who had a good job and provided well for her. Before that she had traveled often to villages to tell them about her Savior, Jesus, and what he meant to her, and what He could do for them.

What could a beautiful, healthy, smiling young woman tell hardened poverty-stricken people about love and about a God who wanted to "lift them out of a pit," as she often described their condition?

Penninah would often tell them a story of a desperately poor woman, whose heart was filled with evil. She told of how the woman had given birth to a child, but was either unable because of her poverty or unwilling because of her wickedness to bring up the child properly. Instead, Penninah would tell them, the woman took the child out into a field, dug a shallow hole, buried the child alive, and walked away.

Perhaps such a thing happened often, so the village people were not impressed by that part of the story. Penninah went on to tell about a pack of dogs who surrounded the buried child and tried to dig it up, barking and barking—so much that a man heard the dogs and went to see what they were trying to dig up out of the ground. Pushing the dogs aside, he then noticed a tiny arm, and thought it was an old doll someone had buried. Digging further, he found that it was wrapped in a rag. Finally he pulled the whole bundle out of the ground and discovered the child.

Looking up, the man saw a woman nearby and called to her. "We must get the child to a hospital," the woman said. "I believe she is still alive." They thought of the Ramabai Mukti Mission nearby and quickly took the child there.

At the mission, a missionary looked at the baby girl, covered with dirt and asked, "How did this happen?"

Tears filled the missionary's eyes as she thought of the sad scene of a woman burying her own child. "We must find the mother," she said. "Go and call the police."

When the policeman came and heard the story, he went to the place where the child was found. After some investigation, he learned who the mother was and brought her to the hospital. "Why did you bury your child?" he asked her. "Don't you love her?" The woman sat scowling, refusing to answer.

The policeman became cross. "You stay here and take care of your baby, or we will put you in jail."

Then Penninah told the people that the woman stayed a few hours, but she soon disappeared leaving the child in the care of the hospital staff. "When the child became healthy, they placed her in the Ramabai Mukti orphanage. The child grew up, and as a young girl she learned about the love of Jesus and saw that kind of love being shown to her," Penninah explained.

"Ask me why I tell you the story of such a pitiful little girl who was pulled out of a pit, and I will tell you," Penninah said. "I was that child!"

Looking Inward: And so were all of us. The Psalmist wrote: "He also brought me up out of a horrible pit, out of the miry clay, and set my feet upon a rock, and established my steps" (Psalm 40:2). Looking Inward, we must never forget what God did for us when he delivered us from the dungeon of sin.

Looking Outward: The Psalmist continued: "He has put a new song in my mouth — praise to our God; many will see it and fear, and will trust in the Lord" (Psalm 40:3). If others don't hear what God has done for us, they may stay in their pits forever.

W.W.
Ramabai Mukti Mission

Twenty-nine

Bong and
The Polka-dot Shirt

Philippines

> There is nothing so small or apparently indifferent which God does not ordain or permit even to the fall of a leaf. —Jean-Pierre de Caussade, *Treatise*

Missionaries Barbara and Jim Hibschman had come to America on furlough. Before they returned to the Philippines, they left instructions that made one American very happy. As soon as he found time, he went to his closet, pulled out that shirt he didn't like, and dropped it in a bag. He hadn't liked it from the start when he received it as a gift. Now he heard he could put it in a parcel the church was sending overseas to the Hibschmans. He felt he could, with a clear conscience, be rid of the ugly thing forever.

After a few weeks, the parcel containing the shirt and other materials the church brought together for the occasion was wrapped and mailed. He was glad to see it go.

For the next few months the package lay in the darkness of a mailbag in the hold of a ship, making its way across the Pacific Ocean to the Philippines.

For the next weeks, the large parcel was sent from one place to another in the mail distribution system until it arrived in a remote village of the Philippines.

By then the Hibschmans were back in their place of ministry. They had worked for weeks with a group of Filipino young people, preparing them for a gospel program they were going to present in the downtown plaza. Everyone was excited except Bong, a fourteen-year-old. Bong had a beautiful voice, and the missionaries had given him a solo part to sing. The Teen Singers were going to dress alike, wearing white trousers and shirts made out of blue with white polka dots.

Jim noticed that Bong had become quiet and despondent. He was always shy, but they knew something was wrong. They learned that Bong had no money, and he had not been able to afford the blue and white material from which to have his shirt made.

"Let Nonoy sing my part," he said, trying to get out of appearing in public wearing something different than the other young people. "He can sing it well."

"We can loan you the money, Bong," Barbara insisted. "You can work during Christmas vacation and earn enough to pay us back." Bong finally agreed. The couple could sense the struggle. He didn't want to be different from his friends; yet he didn't want to admit he was too poor to buy what others could buy.

Thinking they had solved the problem Jim and Barbara went to the local market where the material was sold. They looked everywhere but didn't find any of the same material. They went to shop after shop, and each time the vendors shook their heads. "Perhaps you should try the barter market," one said. They went to the area where people swapped one type of goods for another, but with no success.

When material appeared in the markets, it came in large bolts. When a particular kind was sold, it might never appear in the market again. That is what had happened with the blue and white polka dot material.

The couple returned to the school and tried to persuade Bong to take his singing part anyway, urging him to wear his white shirt and stand behind some of the other boys. Sadly, he agreed to do so, but they sensed how badly he felt.

After rehearsal, the couple started home, stopping at the post office on the way. Bong's problem had been a big disappointment to them as well, for they had prayed all afternoon as they scoured the market trying to find the material. It seemed a cruel trick to play on a young Filipino lad who was already struggling with his faith.

Then Jim came back to the car, carrying a large package which he handed to Barbara. "Why, it's from the church where we spoke the month before we left America!" she said.

Back home they were excited as they opened the package, hoping for the usual Pringle's potato chips, nylon stockings, candy, cake mixes, and other goodies that usually came for Christmas.

They found many things they were looking for. And they also found a bag of used clothing, usually not anything too special or exciting. But then they started to pull out the items of clothing, one by one. Near the bottom of the bag was a blue and white polka dot shirt, the exact same material as the other boys had made into shirts for their appearance in the plaza.

"Barbara," Jim said, looking at the post mark on the package. "Do you realize what God did? Four months before we prayed for that material, God had someone back in America put this shirt in a parcel to send to us."

They couldn't wait until Bong could see the shirt. And it was a perfect fit!

The next week the plaza was filled with the bright sounds of gospel music coming from the Teen Singers. One clear sweet teen-aged voice seemed to stand out above all the others.

Looking Inward: Jesus assured His followers, "For your heavenly Father knows that you need all these things" (Matthew 6:32). The One who created the universe knows also our needs. When we become His, our problems become His problems.

Looking Outward: We never know, when God inclines us to some action, however illogical it may seem, what He has planned. Sometimes even our foolishness can result in God's blessing to others. How much more blessed it is, when out of our desire to please Him, we choose to enter into His work to bring blessing to others!

W.W.
Philippine Evangelical Enterprises, Inc.

Thirty

Rosey
Life on the Streets

Sri Lanka

A bird doesn't sing because he has an answer — he sings because he has a song. —Joan Anglund

---

Ten-year-old Rosey snapped her fingers in time to the American Negro spiritual she sang as the van bumped along the winding road. We were traveling from Sri Lanka's capital city, Colombo, to the city of Kandy. It was a Saturday outing for her and other children from Lotus Buds Children's Home. The children sang as the van rumbled through rain forests, beside rice paddies and coconut palm groves on the way to the mountain resort two hours away. Small cottages nestled in the lush undergrowth. Roadside vendors sold pineapples, bananas, and avocados to people in the passing cars.

Dark brown eyes shone beneath Rosey's jet-black straight bangs. Her pixie face was framed by short bobbed hair. Assuming the role of little mother, Rosey handed out peanuts, candy, and drinks of water to the other children in the van.

Although the language spoken in the orphanage is Sinhala, the official language of Sri Lanka, the children learn English by singing English praise hymns. Rosey's native language was Tamil, but she had become fluent in Sinhala and English during the year she had lived at Lotus Buds.

Rosey told me she had spent her first nine years living on the streets of Jaffna, a city two hundred miles north of Colombo. I remembered from studying Sri Lanka's history that during the years of British rule, Tamils were imported from southern India to work the tea plantations located near Jaffna in the northern part of the island. When Sri Lanka (formerly Ceylon) became independent in 1948 and Sinhala became the official language, riots erupted between the Tamils and the Sinhalese. In modern times, attempts by the ruling Buddhist Sinhalese majority to repatriate these Hindu Tamils has caused bitterness and warfare. The plantation Tamils have not gained Sri Lankan citizenship, nor are they economically well off today.

"Eelam," a Tamil cry of independence for Jaffna and the northern region has echoed through the streets ever since. Any random act by an extremist sends Buddhists and Hindus marching. Hundreds have been killed in this never-ending religious war.

A scar running from Rosey's arm, to her side, and down her leg serves as a grim reminder of past days for this little girl. When I pointed to the scar, she said nonchalantly, "A van hit me." Unlike most of the children in the Lotus Buds Children's Home, Rosey is not really an orphan. Her mother abandoned the family when the child was six. Her father tried to make a living for Rosey and her many brothers and sisters by repairing umbrellas at a stand on a street corner in downtown Jaffna. He could have made more money begging, but Rosey's father was too proud to beg. They lived nearby in a rusted corrugated iron shanty that opened on a main street.

Often in the evenings, Rosey's father and his children gathered around a friend's transistor radio. One night an announcer on a Tamil program beamed from the Seychelles spoke of Christ and of eternal life for those who believe in Him. Rosey's father decided to visit a nearby Christian church. Eventually he began to attend regularly.

At the age of eight, Rosey developed asthma. The exhaust fumes from passing cars made her breathing difficult, and free medicine could only be obtained at the government hospital a long distance away. Her father wondered how much longer he could care for his suffering daughter. Then came the day when she ran out in the street and was hit by a van. Something needed to be done. After she was released from the hospital, he contacted his pastor and asked, "Could you find a home for Rosey? I love her, but I cannot care for her many needs any longer."

The pastor wrote to Therese at Lotus Buds Children's Home, and arrangements were made for Rosey to move to Colombo. The orphanage is run by an American woman whom the children look to as a mother. Six Sinhalese Christian women work and live at Lotus Buds. They sleep and eat in the same rooms with the children.

Despite the loving, home-like environment, Rosey felt abandoned, not understanding why her father had taken her two hundred miles from home to live among strangers. But soon she grew to love Therese, the other women, and the children in the orphanage. She played with and fed the toddlers and led them in singing.

Every few months, Rosey's father visited her in Colombo. One day he moved her younger sister, Sudhi, to Lotus Buds to join her. When the time came for their father to catch the train back to Jaffna, Rosey threw her arms around him and said, "Daddy, don't leave." He held her tightly, but they both knew he must go.

A few weeks later, the civil war in Jaffna intensified. Jaffna fell under a twenty-four hour curfew. The trains stopped running, and Tamil rebels raided many of the food storage areas. Once again, Rosey felt abandoned. "Why doesn't my father come to visit anymore?" she asked Therese. "I miss him."

Therese explained, "Your father loves you and Sudhi very much, but he cannot leave Jaffna as long as the war is raging." Therese read the story of Moses in Exodus 2 to the children one evening. "Pharaoh ordered all the male Hebrew children killed. When Moses' mother feared for his life, she built an ark and hid him in the reeds by the river's bank. Pharaoh's daughter found Moses and raised him as her own son."

Therese turned to Rosey. "Just as Moses' mother was willing to give him up when she feared for his life, your father was willing to send you to Colombo where you would be safe with us. Your father loves you enough to let you go. He loves you enough to allow you to start a new life in a home filled with Christian love and friendship. He wants you to go to school and learn so that you will never have to return to the war-torn streets of Jaffna."

Perhaps someday peace would come to Jaffna, and Rosa and Sudhi could be reunited with their father. In the meantime, she realized that God had given her a new home—one filled with Christian love and singing. As the van continued to bounce along the road to Kandy, Rosey once again turned to her attentive young audience, snapped her fingers, and began singing, "Praise Ye the Lord."

Looking Inward: Many of us go through times when we feel neglected or abandoned—by parents or mates. It is easy for us to turn inward and feel sorry for ourselves. Sometimes we don't understand the motives behind the actions of a loved one, and we feel let down.

Looking Outward: God challenges us to focus on Him rather than on ourselves and our circumstances. He has promised to take care of us. He will never leave us. Although we cannot always comprehend why we have to experience certain difficulties, if we keep our eyes on the Lord, He will walk with us every step of the way.

S.T.O.
Shepherd's Heart Ministries

Thirty-one

Two Rupees for Surakata

Sri Lanka

You can never do a kindness too soon because you never know how soon it will be too late. —Author unknown

---

Surakata was a friendly ten-year old boy, enrolled in the vocational training program at the Sumith Center sponsored by Heart of Compassion ministry. Whenever Deo Miller visited the center on the outskirts of Colombo, Sri Lanka, Surakata greeted him with a wide grin and an update on his weaving project. When the boy first joined the program, he learned to weave place mats. Soon he graduated to his first ten-by-ten floor mat.

Deo enjoyed encouraging the youth who attended the program regularly. On one particular visit, Deo walked into the mat-making room where he expected to be greeted by Surakata with a progress report on his rug mat. However, the boy was not there. Deo asked the director, "Do you know where Surakata is?"

She shrugged her shoulders and replied, "He might be sick, or maybe he's running errands for his mother."

Although regular attendance at the feeding and vocational training centers is stressed to the parents, sometimes they don't understand the importance of a daily commitment to the program. If they need work done at home or help with the younger children, they ask the boy or girl to stay home for a day.

About a week later, Deo and his wife, Elaine, returned to the Sumith Center. Surakata was still missing.

The center leader said, "Deo, we're worried now about Surakata. He attended regularly. It's not like him to be absent over a week. If I give you directions to his home, will you stop by this afternoon?"

Deo nodded. He and Elaine climbed in a van and instructed the driver, who drove them through the lush jungle growing along the riverside. The narrow road wound back and forth, following the meandering river to the village where Surakata lived.

The driver parked. Deo walked up the crooked trail leading to the village. A woman, who was washing her clothes in the river, directed him to the hut where Surakata lived. Surakata's mother sat outside the shanty. She rocked back and forth, tightly clutching her knees in her arms. A low moan escaped from her lips. Tears streamed down her cheeks.

Deo walked up to her and placed his hand on her shoulder. "Hello. I'm Deo Miller from the Sumith Center. We've missed Surakata. Where is he?"

"He's terribly sick," was the mother's tired response. "I don't know what's wrong with him."

"Where is he?" Deo repeated.

"He's lying inside on the floor," she answered, motioning to the entrance of her home.

Deo entered the hot, musty hut, bending down as he walked through the low doorway. When his eyes became adjusted to the dark interior, he saw Surakata curled up on a mat in the corner. His body was contorted into an unnatural position. Deo tried to speak to him, but the boy didn't respond. His forehead burned with fever.

Picking up the semiconscious boy, mat and all, Deo carried him out of the stifling hut. He laid the boy gently on the ground near his mother. Surakata remained in the strange, fetal position, unable to move or communicate.

"How long has he been like this?" Deo asked.

"Almost a week. I can't break the fever." The mother's penetrating eyes searched the American's for reassurance. She asked, "Will Surakata die?"

Deo could not meet her gaze. Instead, he stared in horror at the distorted figure. "I'll take him to the hospital. I have a car here. Do you have a blanket that I can wrap him in?"

The woman entered her house and returned with a tattered piece of fabric. Deo wrapped the frail body and gently lifted Surakata into his arms. Carefully he hiked down the winding path to the van.

When the driver saw the seriousness of the situation, he gunned the engine, winding through the traffic in the make-shift ambulance.

A nurse greeted them at the emergency entrance of the large, white government hospital. Upon seeing the boy, she shook her head. "No hope, no hope."

Ignoring her diagnosis, Deo signed the necessary forms to admit the gravely ill boy for treatment. Then, he and Elaine returned to their flat, leaving Surakata in the hands of God and the hospital staff.

Deo and Elaine often prayed for this friendly little boy until Deo found time to visit Surakata again. Entering the government hospital, he discovered a maze of corridors with no central information center and no signs. However, he knew there must be a children's ward. He wound his way through building after building, wing after wing. At first, he did not see any nurses or children. An overflow of beds spilled into the hallways. Apparently every bed was filled, because many patients reclined on mats on the floor.

Finally, Deo located a nurse in a large ward on the third floor. She motioned down another corridor and pointed upstairs. When he reached the end of the hallway, he heard the chatter and laughter of children, filtering down the staircase. He climbed the stairs to the fourth floor where he finally found the children's area.

The place reeked of Lysol. There were no doors on the rooms. Each ward contained twenty-five to thirty beds. The iron-rail frames, painted white long ago, were cracked and peeling. Thin, two-inch mattresses rested on the metal frames.

Few children were in bed. Most ran up and down the halls, acting as if they were out for recess. Deo saw no nurses.

Deo walked into the next ward and finally found a nurse who knew Surakata. She said, "He had an attack of rheumatic fever. He is weak, so we suspect there is a hole in his heart. He needs total bed rest and no activity for many months."

She showed Surakata's bed to Deo. It was empty. They found him in the hall, chasing another boy. Deo gave the nurse a disapproving glance. Then he noticed her lined face and wondered what working in this bedlam would be like.

The nurse shrugged her stooped shoulders and said flatly, "I have fifty children to take care of by myself. I do the best I can."

Deo took Surakata by the hand and led him back to his bed. He gently said, "Surakata, I'm glad you feel better, but you look tired."

He nodded in agreement.

Deo continued, "The only way you will get well is to take care of yourself. You have to rest in bed all the time until you are strong. When you feel better, you can return to the Sumith Center. But you must do your part."

Sitting on the edge of the bed, Deo hugged this special boy. The doctor's report stated that Surakata's eyes had crossed due to the muscle spasms and fever. Deo knew this condition would probably never be corrected, but at least he was alive.

Six weeks later, the hospital released the young boy. Deo visited his home and emphasized the doctor's advice to his mother. "Surakata can't fetch water from the river or carry firewood. Making him do heavy labor of any kind will kill him. His older sister can bring food home from the center for him each day."

His mother nodded and said, "I promise to let him rest. My husband left us last year. It is difficult to get the chores done, but the other children can help. I want my son to live."

Deo stared at her, trying to phrase his next words. He knew Surakata had been in the feeding and training program at the center for almost six months. "When Surakata first became sick, why didn't you tell someone at the center? Why didn't you do something?"

She looked guilty and hung her head. "He was sick before, but he always got well. I gave him the herbs from the priest, but this time they didn't help. He burned up with fever. He got sicker."

"We told you to come to the center whenever you have a problem. Why didn't you come?"

The mother shook her head. Sickness was a way of life in her village. "I didn't want to bother them. I thought the herbs would make him well."

Deo shivered. The folk religion of the Sinhalese people blends with their Buddhist faith. They worship an assortment of local gods, the most dramatic of which involves the exorcism of demons and spirits, believed to be the cause of disease. Magical practices, enhanced by elaborate dancing and drum rituals, are used by local priests.

Exasperation welled up in Deo as he watched the reaction of Surakata's mother. "Why didn't you take him to the hospital? Why didn't you catch a bus to the government hospital? Treatment is free only a few miles away!"

She hung her head again and mumbled something.

"I can't hear you," he persisted. "Why didn't you take your ill son to the hospital?"

Her sad eyes met the American's gaze as she softly replied, "I would have taken him, but I didn't have two rupees."

Suddenly Deo understood. The bus fare to the hospital was one rupee each way.

Surakata almost died because his mother did not have eight cents for bus fare.

Looking Inward: One day while trying to put coins in a parking meter, a dime slipped from my hand and rolled under my car. As I shrugged my shoulders and walked away, I thought of how much a dime meant to Surakata and how little it meant to me.

Looking Outward: Today I think of how Surakata almost died for a lack of eight cents. I wonder how many other children will die in poverty from a lack of an eight cent bus fare to the hospital.

S.T.O.
Heart of Compassion
Story adapted from *You Start with One* by Deo Miller with Susan F. Titus, published by Thomas Nelson Pub., 1990.

Thirty-two

The Scar
Of Indra

South
Africa

If a man in truth *wills* the Good then he must be willing to suffer *for* the God —Soren Kierkegaard, *Purity of Heart*

Shivering in the bitterly cold apartment, Indra pulled her thin sweater snugly around her shoulders. Snow had fallen on the mountains outside of town. Indra had never seen snow because it seldom occurred in South Africa.

She had cooked breakfast for her husband, Rajah, an hour earlier. After breakfast, her two older children left for school. Indra locked the aluminum door to their clean little one-bedroom apartment.

She turned and looked around at their old portable kerosene heater. She knew she would miss it today, but they couldn't afford kerosene for it during this harsh winter.

Suddenly, Indra's six-month old baby girl, Deviki, began crying. "I'm coming, little one," Indra called out. She walked over to the double bed and slipped beneath the covers to comfort and keep her daughter warm. "Hush now," Indra soothed.

Soon little Deviki drifted back to sleep, but Indra remained wide awake. She had a lot to think about. Life was turning out so differently than she had planned. She had always hoped that someday she would be a famous seamstress. Instead she married an extremely cruel older man. He wasted money on alcohol, refusing to share enough to buy even a small piece of material to sew, something that would brighten her dreary days.

In the midst of feeling sorry for herself, to her utter horror, she saw a stranger walk right through her locked front door. He had black hair and wore a long black robe. He stood and stared at her. He did not speak.

I'm going mad, Indra thought. *This can't be happening. No one can walk through a locked door.*

Just then the black-garbed man took a step toward her. She screamed. Deviki woke and began crying. "Get out of here," Indra yelled at the intruder. "You'd better leave before my husband finds you!"

The man slowly and silently moved closer.

"Help! Who are you?" Indra screamed.

The man took another step and reached for her neck

Indra's breath came in great gulps. Unexpectedly, a name Indra had heard only once came to her mind. When she was a girl of eight, someone had mentioned the name of Jesus. She did not know who Jesus was, but the person who talked about Him spoke with such reverence that Indra was deeply impressed. Not knowing why, she began screaming, "Jesus! Help me, Jesus!"

Immediately, the intruder stopped.

Trembling, Indra repeated, "Jesus! Jesus! Jesus, Help!" To her total astonishment, the man vanished. She held her breath, afraid he would return. But he didn't.

Indra remained in bed for hours, her whole body trembling. *No one will believe this happened, not even my Hindu husband,* she thought. *I can hardly believe it myself. Who was that man? Could he have been a bad spirit? And who is this Jesus? And why is there such power in His name?* Indra sighed. But there was no one to tell her.

Months dragged into years, and the strange intruder experience was almost forgotten. Indra and Rajah began to have terrible fights. Rajah yelled and locked Indra in the bathroom.

Years later Rajah, Indra, and their three children moved into a small house in town. Some of their Indian neighbors brought over a delicious curry dinner to welcome them. When the visitors left, Indra walked out and stood talking on the lawn between their homes.

"Would you like to come next week to a free crochet lesson?" the Christian neighbor asked. "I'm learning to make a shawl. You are welcome to come with me. Maybe you would like to learn to make a doily, a tablecloth, or maybe even a sweater."

Indra's heart beat faster. "It sounds wonderful."

The Christian neighbor said nervously, "This crochet class is taught by a missionary lady. She gives free lessons, but she wants everyone to stay for a Bible story. She's telling about the Christian God and His Son, Jesus."

Indra gasped. It was the first time she had heard the name Jesus since that horrible day, five years earlier.

The week could not pass quickly enough for Indra. To learn how to crochet was like a dream come true, and to hear about this Jesus who she had once called upon for help was even better.

Irene Quick, a missionary with African Evangelical Fellowship, was in her early sixties. Her soft gray curls framed a kind smiling face as she demonstrated how to properly hold the crochet hook with fingers bent by painful arthritis.

After a few simple instructions, Miss Quick walked around the circle of ladies to see how each was progressing. When she came to Indra she stopped and said, "My goodness, you're doing so well. It will be no time before you are able to crochet a sweater for your little daughter." The missionary smiled and reached out to give Deviki a gentle hug.

A lump formed in Indra's throat. It had been years since she had heard a kind word or felt a loving touch. Many fights with Rajah had turned their home into a place of violence.

After the crochet lesson, the Bible story began. Using a large board, draped with a piece of flannel over it, the missionary used colorful pictures to tell a story about how God made the world. She ended by quoting John 3:16: "For God so loved the world that He gave His only begotten Son, that whoever believes in Him should not perish but have everlasting life."

Truths about Jesus, the Son of God, and His love brought tears to Indra's eyes. Week after week, Indra and five-year-old Deviki listened intently to the Bible stories.

One night, Indra slipped out from under the covers, trying her best not to disturb her husband or Deviki. She knelt quietly beside her bed, at first fearful of speaking to God. Finally Indra whispered, "I know for sure it was You who saved me years ago from that bad spirit. You did that when I was heavy with sin. I am still heavy with sin. I used to only think of my husband's evil, but now I understand. It is my sin that has come between You and me. Please forgive me. Please God, I want to give you everything... my temper, my hatred, Rajah, everything!"

Quietly, Indra got up and slipped back into bed. Peace descended upon her rigid body, and soon her muscles began to relax. She drifted into a restful sleep.

The next morning after Rajah and the two older children left, Indra rushed out to the tool shed. Returning with a hammer, she began taking down the Hindu prayer altar that stood in the corner of their front room.

"What are you doing, Mummy?" Deviki asked.

Startled, Indra replied, "These images are not real gods. I never want to pray to them again. I'm taking down this shelf and hiding these idols. I want all of this out. From now on, I worship only Jesus"

"I love Him, too," Deviki said.

With tears running down her soft brown cheeks, Indra hugged her daughter. "You are still a little girl. Soon you will start school. I wonder if you really understand."

"I've been listening to the Bible stories, Mummy, and I love Jesus."

That evening when Rajah returned, he had been drinking. He immediately saw that the god-shelf was missing. In a slurred voice he shouted, "What's happened here? Where are my gods?"

Indra lowered her eyes. "I hid them, Rajah. I do not want to pray to them anymore. I know you never say prayers, so I thought you would not mind."

"Wouldn't mind! Of course I mind. Go get them. Bring them back, and fix that shelf. I want you to bow down right now and pray to my gods."

"Please Rajah," Indra said nervously. "Please do not make me. I only want to pray to Jesus."

"Jesus!" Rajah sounded like a madman. "I do not know this Jesus. Get me my gods!"

Rajah turned his drunken wrath on little Deviki. "Where are they? Go and find them!"

"I. . . I don't know where they are," Deviki swallowed nervously. With grave respect, she added softly, "B. . . but please, Father, I. . . I want to pray to Jesus, too."

Rajah shoved Deviki into the corner and told her not to move. Then he turned and grabbed Indra by the hair and slammed her forehead against the headboard of the bed. The skin, above her eye, gashed open and started to bleed. Desperately, Indra pulled away and scrambled under the bed. As she lay in her blood, she began to pray.

Rajah ran to the kitchen to get a butcher knife. He yelled, "I'm going to finish what I've started."

"Jesus! Jesus!" Indra cried. "Please hold the door closed and don't let Rajah kill me. And please protect little Deviki." From under the bed, Indra could see that the bedroom door hung open about one inch, and all it needed was a simple push.

Rajah came back with the knife and kicked the door with his foot. It did not budge. He put his fingers around the edge of the door and pushed with all his strength. "I don't know how you're keeping me from coming in, but you'd better stop!"

"Jesus!" Indra kept crying. "Please keep Your hand on that door. I am Yours to save. Years ago You rescued me from that bad spirit. I know You can save us now."

Unable to open the door, Rajah finally passed out and fell to the floor. When Indra heard the knife drop, she crawled out from under the bed and pushed open the bedroom door. As she and her daughter stood over Rajah's sleeping form, Indra was surprised at her own feelings. Instead of thinking of ways to get even with her husband, she found herself praying for him.

The gash in her forehead, now covered with dried blood, would leave an ugly scar. "I don't mind," Indra said. "It will remind me of how God answered our prayers."

Looking Inward: We all carry scars from the past. Some are visible like Indra's, and some are inside of us seen only by God. Paul reminded Timothy that "all who desire to live godly in Christ Jesus will suffer persecution" (2 Timothy 3:12). God doesn't always keep us from getting hurt, but He shows us He really cares.

Looking Outward: Indra's road to faith in Christ has been rough and long. Her future may not be easy either. But suffering for Christ is nothing to shun. Paul called it a privilege: "For to you it has been granted on behalf of Christ, not only to believe in Him, but also to suffer for His sake" (Philippians 1:29). But like Indra, we now have One who suffers with us—One who cares.

S.T.O.
African Evangelical Fellowship (AEF)

Thirty-three

Chaya
From Shadow to Sunshine

India

Behind the dim unknown,
Standeth God within the shadow,
Keeping watch above his own.
—James Russell Lowell, *The Present Crisis*

"Here is a gift for you," the nurse said, handing a bundle to Sugandhi, the sick room nurse at the Ramabai Mukti Mission orphanage.

"Oh no," Sugandhi said, when she saw the sickly child.

"You must take her," the nurse said, "We can't take care of her at the hospital anymore." She then told Sugandhi that the little girl, more than three years old, weighing less than ten pounds was named "Chaya." When her parents brought her to the hospital, she was so sick and malnourished no one thought she would live more than a few days.

Chaya means "shadow," and that was what she looked like—a vanishing shadow. With listless eyes, pale skin, twig-like hands and feet, she looked as if she might fade away at any time. Her puffy stomach itself was a sign of malnutrition. It was all Sugandhi could do to keep from crying when she pushed back the blanket and saw the tiny little frame she held in her arms.

The doctor who visited the sick room shook his head when he saw her. "She will need a lot of care. Feed her small quantities of food and milk," he said as he wrote out a prescription for vitamins.

Feeding Chaya was a task. After months of neglect and misery, Chaya was distrustful.

"Come, precious Sonu, (meaning "gold" in the Marathi language), you must eat," Sugandhi cooed.

"Nakho!" ("Don't want!") Chaya would scream back.

But Sugandhi was discovering a truth about God-given love others have learned: You cannot bear the burdens of another without beginning to love the one you are trying to help.

The orphanage was arranged so that children were placed in small groups as family units. Soon the doctor was trying to move Chaya out into one of the "families" where they had handicapped children, since Chaya, though nearly four, was unable to walk.

"But doctor," Sugandhi protested, "please let us try physical therapy and see if she can learn to walk."

Needing often to invent games to entice Chaya to eat, Sugandhi began to play one of Chaya's favorites, "The Crow."

"Sonu, show me how the crow opens its mouth. What does the crow say?"

"Caw! Caw!" Chaya opened her mouth to imitate the crow. Down went the food! Enjoying all the fuss and attention, love began to win over the child who seemed to have lost the will to live.

"God, please touch her and heal her. Make her walk," Sugandhi prayed day after day.

Soon Chaya weighed fourteen pounds. Her eyes brightened and she learned to smile. God answered Sugandhi's prayers one by one.

Later the little girl graduated to one of the families and learned to walk, first with a little walker. Before too many months she was running with the other children, swinging on the monkey bars in the play area.

The power of faith, trusting in a powerful, loving God, and the power of love, both God's and Nurse Sugandhi's, brought life out of death, hope out of despair, Sonu (golden sunshine) out of Chaya (shadow).

Looking Inward: Until Jesus came, all of our lives were filled with darkness inside. The Apostle Paul wrote: "For you were once darkness, but now you are light in the Lord. Walk as children of light" (Ephesians 5:8).

Looking Outward: Jesus said, "I must work the works of Him who sent Me while it is day; the night is coming when no one can work. As long as I am in the world, I am the light of the world" (John 9:4, 5). On another occasion, Jesus said, to us his disciples, "You are the light of the world . . . Let your light so shine before men, that they may see your good works and glorify your Father in heaven" (Matthew 5:14-16).

W.W.
Ramabai Mukti Mission

Thirty-four

The Spear
And the Scalpel

Zambia

Never be afraid to trust an unknown future to a known God. —Corrie ten Boom

---

Dr. Robert Foster leaned over the examining table in Mutanda, Zambia in Africa. He had arrived just before noon. After a quick lunch, he rushed to the clinic and the work at hand. Several hundred people sat outside the door in the hot African sun, a hundred of them patients, lined up to see him.

Wiping his brow with the back of his hand, Bob turned his attention to his first patient, the woman lying on the table, and began examining her.

Suddenly, in the middle of the examination, she sat up and pulled her cloth around her. "I have to leave," she stammered as she started climbing off the table.

"But I'm not finished yet," replied the bewildered doctor.

The woman shouted, "No. I want to leave!"

Bob continued to listen to her heart and realized it was racing wildly. What was going on? He straightened up and looked quizzically at the woman.

She immediately jumped off the table and ran. As soon as she reached the door, she shouted, "Don't anybody go into the clinic. There's a big snake in there."

Bob turned and looked around, but he didn't see any snake. So he followed the woman outside and asked, "Where is the snake?" I don't see anything."

She replied, "Kahaya, when I was lying down on your examining table, I looked up at the rafters. A big black mamba hung right above your head."

The doctor once again entered the clinic door and looked up into the thatched roof. There he saw the mamba, as thick as his arm and at least eight feet long, lying on the rafter at the gable end of the roof.

He knew no patients could safely enter that room again, nor could he, until that snake was killed. He returned to the crowd outside and asked, "Who will help me kill the snake?"

Silence filled the air. Not one of the hundreds sitting there volunteered.

Again Bob asked, "Who will help me? We've got to kill it. We can't work as long as that snake's in there."

Again no one responded.

Finally the pastor who had come to hold a meeting with the patients while they waited replied, "Kahaya, you go. We'll pray."

Taken back for a moment, Bob agreed. "All right. If you'll pray, I'll go. Does anyone have a gun?"

They all shook their heads. Then one man came forward with a six-foot long spear. "You can fight the mamba with this."

Another fellow handed the doctor a cane. So armed with a spear and a cane, Bob stepped back into the dark empty clinic— empty except for that slithering mass of death, now watching him menacingly. Bob knew if he came within reach, the snake would bury his deadly fangs in him instantly, and he'd never make it out alive. Someone brought a step ladder so that Bob could get near enough to strike the snake with the spear.

Bob analyzed his chances. "If I get him speared against the wall, I can hit him with the cane."

He called outside to the people, "OK, now you pray."

With a crescendo of prayer outside, Bob hit the mamba in the middle of its body, pinning it to the wall. In a flash, the venomous head attacked, missing him by inches. With his right hand, Bob swung the heavy cane, intending to strike the snake's head. But the creature struck so quickly, the cane missed. Over and over again, Bob and the serpent lashed out at each other. Because his body was held by the spear, the snake could not reach Bob. And each time the deadly head managed to duck Bob's every blow.

The prayers outside the window continued unabated as the man and snake held each other at bay for over an hour. Eventually Bob's arm holding the spear became so tired, he could not continue. With a jerk, he pulled the spear out of the wall and threw the snake to the ground. The mambo disappeared behind a cupboard. Gingerly Bob climbed down from the ladder and stepped outside. All eyes were on him.

"Look," he pleaded, "I'm tired. The snake's tired. It's gone behind the cupboard. I need some help to finish him off." Again his plea was met with silence. Then a wizened old man with a crippled leg came forward to help. He was so short, he fit under Bob's arm.

The two of them returned to the scene of battle. Bob explained that if they pushed the cupboard against the wall, the snake would try to dart out. If he escaped, it would be the end of them. But if they held the cupboard tightly against the wall, the snake would be stuck part way out.

At Bob's shout, the two slammed the cupboard against the wall, and the deadly head emerged. As Bob predicted the mamba could move no further. Bob struck the gigantic snake in the head. Several mighty wallops finished the job.

In the days that followed, Bob often drew a parallel between the story and missionary work. "People say to me, `Bob, you go. We'll pray.' And I say that if they really pray, God will work." He found, too, that when it comes to volunteering for difficult ministry, often the old and decrepit are willing while the youthful and seemingly strong-hearted hold back.

Looking Inward: It is easy to come up with excuses for not responding to God's call to help others. Sometimes we think we are not talented enough or qualified for a certain responsibility. But God promises to provide the skills we need if we will step out in faith and trust Him.

Looking Outward: We can put off indefinitely serving the Lord in action by telling others, "You go. I'll pray for you." Often we think that certain talents or knowledge are necessary for becoming involved in Christian ministry. Yet, perhaps the Lord is telling us that He wants us to serve Him just as we are.

S.T.O.
African Evangelical Fellowship (AEF)
Story adapted from *Sword and Scalpel* by Lorry Lutz, published by Promise Pub., 1990, used with permission.

Thirty-five

Marcel's Story
The Train Ride

France

What we practice, not (save at rare intervals) what we preach, is usually our great contribution to the conversion of others. —C. S. Lewis, *Letters of C.S. Lewis*

A group of Operation Mobilization team members were gathered, and several reported on their efforts. Marcel shared a story that could have explained how many of them had felt at times.

She had been on the train coming to the meeting, thinking about the report she would give. She had looked forward to the time alone. Settling into a nice comfortable seat, she was lost in thought when a young woman, in her early twenties, sat down beside her.

Oh, no! she thought. *I hope she doesn't want to talk.*

Sure enough, the girl smiled as she sat down and exchanged friendly greetings. Marcel greeted her back, but ended her words with that and turned back to the notebook in front of her.

"Would you like to read some of my newspapers?" the girl asked. "I have finished with them. You can have them if you like."

"No, thank you," Marcel answered and returned to her notebook.

The train rolled on for a few miles, and Marcel was again lost in concentration about her reports.

"Would you like some chewing gum? I have more. Please take some if you like," the girl said with a friendly smile.

"No, thank you," Marcel answered, in a friendly tone, but not quite as friendly as before.

Is she going to talk like this all the way? Marcel wondered.

Each time Marcel looked at the girl, she smiled broadly at her, as if hoping Marcel would say something. After a while the girl settled back, opened the satchel she was carrying and took out a walk-man tape player. Adjusting the headphones, she picked up her newspaper. Marcel seemed released from the burden of having to speak to her.

Several minutes later, Marcel glanced at the girl, who immediately whipped off the earphones, as if hoping her seat-mate would say something to start a conversation. When Marcel turned away, the headphones went back on and the girl returned to her newspaper.

This isn't right, Marcel thought. She knew God wanted her to be more zealous. The girl beside her, in fact, looked more poised than she herself felt. *Why has God brought me to this place, anyway?* she asked herself. Then, tearing a sheet from her notebook, she wrote: "Mademoiselle, do you believe in God?" She placed the note on the newspaper in the girl's lap from which she was reading.

The girl read the note, and in a flash, removed the headphones. Her face broadened into a smile, as if happy to be able at last to talk to Marcel. "What do you mean?" she asked.

Putting away her notebook, Marcel explained her question. Turning toward each other in the broad seat, a conversation began between the two young women. Long explanations, wide-eyed attention, and many more questions and explanations from the Bible Marcel now held in her lap resulted.

The next half hour seemed like only minutes, as Marcel shared the Good News about a God of love.

Like Philip of old, as he rode in the chariot of the Ethiopian to whom God had directed him, she was talking to one who would never understand unless someone guided her. "Then Philip opened his mouth, and beginning at this Scripture, preached Jesus to him" (Acts 8:35).

Philip had been busy preaching the gospel when the Holy Spirit directed him to approach the chariot. And here, on another day, riding in a different kind of "chariot," someone who bore the Good News about Jesus was able to share it. On that particular train, to that particular coach, to that particular seat, the Holy Spirit had directed a young French woman to sit and hear the Good News.

Looking Inward: At times when we are most concerned about ourselves, the Holy Spirit might be most concerned about someone He wants to send our way.

Looking Outward: All the Holy Spirit asked of Marcel, and all He asks of any of us, is to be ready with the Message, at the right time, in the right place, to the right person. The Holy Spirit can do the rest.

W.W.
Operation Mobilization (OM)

Thirty-six

Nails
For Yelwa's Bowl Covers

Niger
Republic

Teach us, good Lord, to serve Thee as Thou deservest.
To give and not to count the cost:
To fight and not to heed the wounds:
To toil and not to seek for rest:
To labour and not to ask for any reward
Save that of knowing that we do thy will.
—St. Ignatius Loyola, *Prayer for Generosity*

"Nails for her bowl covers?" my wife asked. "What do you suppose she wants?"

Yelwa, the wiry little widow, turned to me and smiled, thinking perhaps I would understand her Hausa language better. She repeated it to me, *"K'usar fai-fai."* She looked disappointed that I didn't understand either.

Finally she tried again, "You know, nails for the bowl covers that tell people about Jesus."

The light dawned. "Nails" —she wanted phonograph needles! The bowl covers—well, the big Gospel Recording records did look a little like the round thatched bowl covers the local women made.

Several months before we had given her a cleverly designed phonograph that could be turned by spinning the finger around in a little crank-like device sitting on the top of the recording. Yelwa was Hausa, but from her milk chocolate skin, she looked as if she could have been part Fulani also. We had given her a whole series of Hausa and Fulani recordings of gospel presentations.

While I was back in the house looking for the needles, she explained to my wife that there was a Fulani village about six miles from our town. She had decided to visit a woman she had met at the medical clinic we ran there on the edge of the Sahara Desert in southern Niger Republic.

Late that afternoon we heard her soft call at the back door again.

This time she brought another request. Typically, she went through long greetings before she got around to the real purpose of her visit. She wanted to know if my wife Priscilla could come with her sometime the next week.

"Is there someone there you want me to meet?" my wife asked.

A quick nod of her head and a sucking in of her breath meant "yes."

"There are seven women," she continued. "When I turned the `bowl cover' for them, they said they wanted to know *Yesu Almasihu* (Jesus the Savior).

One day Jesus sat in the temple court and watched a little woman, a widow I think someone very much like Yelwa. He saw two tiny copper coins go into the horn that collected gifts from the worshippers. Many gifts were dropped in that day, but there was something special about her gift. Jesus said, "This poor widow has put in more than all; for all these out of their abundance have put in offerings for God, but she out of her poverty has put in all the livelihood that she had" (Luke 21:3,4).

This was Yelwa, the dried up little widow who often sat by our house and struggled to read even one verse from her Hausa Bible. She came often, but seemed to learn very slowly. This was the old widow everyone had given up on—too old to find another husband, and almost too old to scratch out a little farm with her son-in-law, the pastor.

But she could still sit in her little grass hut on moonless nights and think about villages six miles away. At night she listened to hard blowing rains pounding away on the thatched roof her son-in-law helped buy for her tiny dwelling. Snakes and scorpions sometimes found their way into the rolled up mat that was her bed. But somewhere in the tiny hut, among her handful of belongings, in some dry spot, the stack of dark "bowl covers," were carefully stored. With them, safely tied up in a little piece of cloth, the half-dozen needles I had given her, the "nails" that scratched out an ageless message of love and life.

Looking Inward: Light kept inside our hearts would be as futile as

Looking Inward: Light kept inside our hearts would be as futile as Yelwa's record player if she kept it hidden away in a dark corner of her hut. Even with the little light she had been given, this frail old saint knew that light was meant to be shared.

Looking Outward: The village was six miles away, but it called Yelwa like the voice the Apostle Paul heard in the night, calling him to Macedonia to help them. God doesn't always speak in audible tones to call us to those who need the light, but we must ask ourselves the question: "Would the ears of my heart be open to hear the call if it came?"

W.W.
Gospel Recordings

Thirty-seven

Osuwa
A Place of Refuge

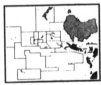

New
Guinea

"How often we look upon God as our last and feeblest resource! We go to Him because we have no where else to go. And then we learn that the storms of life have driven us, not upon the rocks, but into the desired havens. —George Macdonald

---

"Tell me a story," Don Richardson asked of Erariek, a twenty-five-year old Yali man. He was obviously pleased by someone showing interest in him and his people.

The story was an old one—about his brother, Sunahan, and a friend named Kahalek. The two men went out to gather food, according to the story. They were digging sweet potatoes from their garden plot when they heard a noise, an arrow swishing past them. Then suddenly an arrow struck Kahalek. Glancing over their shoulders, the saw a raiding party from another tribe, cannibals from across the Heluk River.

The two man grabbed their bows and arrows and started running. Instead of fleeing up a steep trail toward their village, they turned and ran across their gardens toward a low stone wall. Just as they were about to reach the low wall, another arrow struck Kahalek and he fell, fatally wounded.

Sunahan jumped the wall, whirled around and bared his chest, laughing at the raiders, who stood their distance. By this time people from Sunahan's village heard the commotion, grabbed their weapons, and were streaming down the ridge toward the raiding party.

"But why didn't the raiding party kill Sunahan," Richardson asked.

"You don't understand, Erariek said. "He was standing inside the stone wall."

"What difference did that make?" Richardson asked.

"It was the wall we Yali call *Osuwa*—a place of refuge. If the raiders had shed one drop of Sunahan's blood there, their own people would have been punished with death when they returned home. And Sunahan, though he had a bow and arrows, couldn't shoot at them while he was standing there."

Where had they learned this? And where did the custom arise? he wondered. Was it truths from God buried deep in the hearts of all men? Or was it some carry-over from Jewish customs brought from distant lands in times past?

Their story was strikingly reminiscent of the Jewish cities of refuge. During the early days of Israel, a fugitive who had accidentally killed another person fled to one of the Hebrew towns set aside as a city of refuge. There he was safe—at least until the high priest arbitrated his case. Depending on the results, he could either be set free or be turned over to the avenger of blood to be executed.

Hebrew poets and prophets from that time forward called forward the imagery in such words as "In you, O Lord, I put my trust [have taken refuge in you]; let me never be ashamed" (Psalm 31:1).

Similar stories come from other cultures of a place of refuge, for example the walls of an ancient temple on the western shore of Hawaii. *Pu'uhonua-o-honaunau* was not just another temple. It was a place of refuge for defeated warriors, noncombatants, or "taboo breakers" who reached its boundaries ahead of their pursuers. And *Pu'uhonua-o-honaunau* is said to have been only one of about twenty such cities of refuge scattered over the Hawaiian Islands.

The shadow of truth can only fill the heart with longing. The real truth of God's universal plan is that in Jesus we are offered a place of refuge from the destroyer of our souls, the evil one. The Psalmist wrote: "Bow down your ear to me, Deliver me speedily; Be my rock of refuge, A fortress of defense to save me" (Psalm 31:2).

Looking Inward: Our deepest fears arise when we see the enemy on the outside and fail to see the one who said, "He who is in you is greater than he who is in the world" (1 John 4:4). Today God wants us to see his protecting arm around us and be courageous to face the enemy.

Looking Outward: Seeing a fearful world around us, we need to be heralds of the Good News about the refuge available to us in Jesus Christ. Today can be a new day of demonstrating the courage of a child of God who knows that he is within the reach of his Heavenly Father's protection. Such faith is contagious.

W.W.
Story from *Eternity in Their Hearts* by Don Richardson, Regal Books, 1981, used with permission.

Thirty-eight

Strength
For the Journey

USA

Every day bring God sacrifices and be the priest in this reasonable service, offering thy body and the virtue of thy soul.
—St. John Chrysostom, *A Little Book of Life and Death*

Not a breath of wind stirred the red dust beneath the brush arbor on the Navajo Indian Reservation. It was Sunday evening, and the voice of Pastor Sam was almost as quiet as the night. He told stories of his people—people the seven FACE short-term missionaries grew to love and enjoy during the month they spent in Arizona. They shared the gospel with Navajo children while Pastor Sam conducted evening tent meetings for their parents.

That night, while they were relaxing outside the church, Sam held them spellbound by the following tale.

Almost sixty years ago, when a Navajo named Jim was about ten years old, his grandfather challenged him to a foot race. The bet was that if Jim won, he got to keep the grandfather's horse. If Jim's grandfather won, he received ten sheep.

Now the grandfather was excellent at running short sprints and could have beaten Jim easily at that. However, this was to be a longer race. The distance was the stretch between the church and the windmill in a rocky field about a quarter mile away.

On the day of the race, puffy white clouds contrasted sharply with the intense blue sky and crimson rocks of the mesa near the sheep camp. The boy and his grandfather lined up. The race began.

At first, the runners matched each other step for step along the primitive racetrack. As they drew nearer the goal, the grandfather started panting for breath. They ran on. Even though the grandfather sounded extremely winded, he and his grandson toiled on, side by side. At the very last minute, Jim pulled slightly ahead, winning the race by only a few inches of dusty red ground.

Anger flared in his grandfather's eyes. He turned toward Jim, spitting out the words, "You'll never beat me on those legs again!"

Jim shrugged, claimed his prize, and trotted off on his grandfather's horse. That very hour, while riding home through the sagebrush, Jim's legs started feeling numb. The numbness grew until he could no longer walk at all. His distraught parents consulted several doctors, but each told the boy he had only a year to live. Jim also went to a medicine man, who said that someone close to the paralytic had caused this disaster.

Sometimes a Navajo will act on a grudge by practicing witchcraft against someone in his own family. One type of curse involves burying items under an eagle's nest. The medicine man told Jim to have his friends search for a box containing some of Jim's spittle and dust from one of his footprints. Jim's shepherd friends knew where several eagle nests were located. After hours of searching, they found a buried box containing dust and saliva. They destroyed it, but still Jim did not get well.

The boy weakened day by day, and his parents left him out in the brush arbor to die. One day, he heard beautiful singing coming from the *hogan,* the Navajo meeting house. Missionaries had come to visit his parents.

Jim's father told this Christian couple, "If you want to save someone, go and save my son. He is dying." They walked out to the brush arbor and explained the gospel to Jim. He decided that since he was dying anyway, he might as well try this Jesus. Then, when he died, he would have eternal life. Jim became a Christian.

Not only did the Lord let Jim live, but He has protected Jim's life since then. Once Jim had a serious case of pneumonia and was miraculously healed through prayer.

To this day, Jim travels around the Indian reservation, preaching of God's love and of His power over sickness, witches, and evil spirits.

Pastor Sam told the FACE missionaries more stories about curses being broken, witches becoming Christians, and the sick being healed. At one of Sam's tent meetings, a crippled woman arrived in a wheelchair and asked for prayer. She was concerned that she was becoming a burden to her family, especially during the freezing winter when carrying her to the outhouse was a hardship. That very night, in the blue and white striped tent in the desert, the Lord healed the woman's legs. She can now walk normally and is no longer a burden to her family.

The story about the woman who was healed left one of the short-term missionaries puzzled. "Did the Lord heal the young man called Jim of his paralysis?"

"No," said Pastor Sam, an answer that surprised some of the group, especially after hearing about the woman's healing. Sam's answer was a wise one. Sometimes, hardships are difficult to understand or accept. However, God is more interested in perfecting us for eternity than in making our lives easy now. God doesn't always tell us His reasons for what He does. By helping Jim do what he cannot do for himself, his family and friends are growing in selflessness, practicing the command to consider others more important than themselves. Like the Apostle Paul with his thorn in the flesh, Jim has learned that God's grace is sufficient for him, for power is perfected in weakness.

Looking Inward: The Lord doesn't always answer "yes" to our petitions or give us an explanation. Nevertheless, He does give us strength for the journey and the ability to do all He has set before us. There are things in life that seem to drag us down, like Jim's paralyzed legs. God could change our situation in a second if He chose. Yet after much prayer for relief, His answer for now remains "no." Maybe these difficulties are because God wants to do something special. God's strength seeks to be made perfect in our weakness.

Looking Outward: Sometimes the Lord asks us to serve others in a way that threatens our security. At times, we may feel totally inadequate to do what the Lord has asked of us. When this happens, we can either shrink back as a coward or step forth in God's strength. With God all things are possible.

S.T.O.
Fellowship of Artists for Cultural Evangelism (FACE).

Thirty-nine

The Navajo Shepherd
And His Dream

USA

> We should love [Christ] also because he has loved us. He has run like a shepherd who exhausts himself to find his strayed lamb. After having found us he has taken us and our weakness up himself by taking human form. Fenelon

Kenneth Begishe was born in the 1940s into a traditional Navajo family. His ancestors had survived "The Long Walk" when Kit Carson herded 8,000 of his people into Fort Sumner, New Mexico, keeping them there until their cultural structures could disintegrate.

He went to boarding school run by the Bureau of Indian Affairs, where they "washed out little Navajos' mouths with lye soap" for speaking the Navajo language. "Old Navajo ways are bad," he learned at school before he was ten. "You will never get anywhere until you give them up for the white ways. Then you will have cars and televisions and a good life." These were confusing messages for a good Navajo boy, who had spent long hours sitting with the medicine men, listening to the "sings" (sacred ceremonies), studying the long chants and intricate sand paintings.

The confusing messages sent Kenneth, like many of his friends, to the "anesthetic of choice," the bottle. Soon he was drinking, becoming more and more disruptive with his life. He would go home drunk and pick fights with anyone in sight. He would stagger into a hogan (mud-covered, dome-shaped dwelling) and pull down the wood-stove chimney, sending everyone outside until the smoke cleared. Then he would hide in his mother's hogan until he sobered up, horrified with shame at what he had done.

A turning point came in Kenneth's life in 1960 when Oswald Werner, a young doctoral student, came to live in a guest hogan at the Shonto Trading Post to study the Navajo language. Seeing Kenneth's potential, Oswald invited Kenneth to Chicago in 1963 to help him compile a Navajo medical dictionary. Going to Chicago was an act of desperation for Kenneth. He left because he was too good a Navajo to remain in Navajo country the way he was shaming his people and too bad a drinker to stop.

One night in Chicago, in the middle of a drunker street fight, Kenneth found himself alone in a deserted cemetery, a terrible thing for a Navajo, who won't even remain in a house where someone has died. He ran through the cemetery wildly, looking for an opening in the high iron fence. In his terror he cried out, "God, if you are there, you see where I am. I am going to die if my life goes on this way. So if you want to do something, do it now."

Later, in Oklahoma City, a friend took him to church to hear an evangelist. When the gospel was presented, Kenneth heard God say, "Your prayer in the graveyard is being answered. This is it."

With almost no Bible training Kenneth knew God wanted him to be a pastor among his own people, so he started a small church in his mother's ten-by-ten-foot house. "I didn't know how to be a pastor," Kenneth was heard to say, and later, "I didn't know how to build a church . . . " But soon men showed him how to build the White Post Church, using the inverted cab of an old pickup truck as a cement mixer. One after one, projects got done that Kenneth "didn't know how to do." People showed up from everywhere.

The big denominations built Indian missions in nearby cities and towns, but Kenneth knew that the only way to reach the people was to build churches near where they lived. As soon as a group of ten or more people from a particular area showed up, Kenneth would help them start a church near where they lived and then set about to find a pastor from among them, usually another untrained person like himself. Not that he was against education, but reacting from his own bad experience with "white" education, he felt that they should develop their own leadership for their work. Soon there was a sizable group of Navajo pastors in small churches, scattered all over the reservation.

About that time Kenneth had a very troubling dream. In it he was back herding sheep in the pasture lands as he did as a young boy. He was often scolded if he waited too late to start the sheep back to the sheepfold. In the darkness the sheep could stray and become lost, or wolves would prey on them at night.

In his dream he was trying to herd a large flock of sheep back to the fold, but they were becoming very unmanageable, his fears began to grow, especially when he realized that the small dot on the horizon was actually a ravenous wolf creeping closer and closer.

Nearby a group of young boys played. He called to the boys to help him, and after a while they came. Coming closer, they all had small bodies but their heads and faces were mature men. He asked them to help him form a line so they could begin herding the sheep toward the fold. By that time the wolf was coming closer and closer. Soon he looked around and saw all the boys were back playing again, and the sheep were straying in all directions. Once again he called the sheepherders back again, and this time he said to them, "Take hold of each other's hands." They lined up again, holding hands, and this time were able to get all the sheep moving toward the fold. At that moment, Kenneth awoke from his dream.

For a long time he puzzled over the dream. At the same time the small congregations were drifting into all kinds of problems. For two years Kenneth asked God what he wanted him to do. Eventually he came to understand that the sheepherders were the pastors, and the wandering sheep were the people of their congregations.

The Lord once spoke through Ezekiel: "As a shepherd seeks out his flock on the day he is among his scattered sheep, so will I seek out My sheep and deliver them from all the places where they were scattered" (Ezekiel 34:12). What was needed was someone to get them to "hold hands" and work together. Soon there was a "Fellowship of Ministering Churches," which enabled them to avoid the problems of competition, cliquishness, and power-mongering.

Kenneth doesn't say much at their monthly Saturday morning meetings. They sit around long tables and work their way down a chalkboard agenda that might cover anything from finances to theology.

They are the sheepherders of Kenneth's dream. They are holding hands with each other, directing many sheep into God's fold there in Navajo land.

Looking Inward: We owe our lives to the Good Shepherd; but we are also deeply indebted spiritually to many of God's undershepherds who have cared for our souls. As God's sheep, may we do all we can to obey the voice of God as it comes to us from faithful shepherds.

Looking Outward: The evil one comes, clothed as a wolf, to attack the flock of God. Today God is calling us who know him to "hold hands," to share in the responsibility of shepherding God's flock safely into the fold.

S.T.O.
World Vision
Story from *World Vision* Magazine (June-July 1991), used with permission.

Forty

The Wrong Day
To Go to Allahabad

India

Man writes the almanac, but God makes the weather.
—Dutch proverb

Every day on their four-week trip throughout India, Partners International missionary, Lorry Lutz and Ethel Herr saw God's hand at work. But their last scheduled visit surpassed all.

They planned to spend a weekend in the remote village of Rewa, helping a woman writer named Shanta Arnold with some manuscripts she'd sent to them earlier.

Rewa was located three hours drive from the nearest airport at Allahabad. They realized that the weekend chosen was not the best time to go there, but they didn't know how chaotic it would be. India's largest Hindu festival, the *kumbh mela*, was in progress there. Indians observe the festival in rotation, at four sacred centers, every three years. When it comes to Allahabad, it is extra special, drawing millions of pilgrims from every sect of Hinduism. They come to this spot where three rivers meet, to bathe away their sins and shorten the length of their death-rebirth, or transmigration cycle.

Kumbh mela lasts for two months, with many astrological dates during that time set for pilgrims to take their redemptive dip. But always one date is the most auspicious of all. Further, once every thousand years, planets are lined up in such a way that bathers are assured of reducing their transmigration cycle by 1,000 years!

Lorry and Ethel had no idea, when they headed for Allahabad on a Friday morning, that this special once-every-1,000-year-moment would occur the following Monday!

Sixteen million people descended on Allahabad, many of them arriving at the same time as the two Americans. Transportation, never easy or predictable by American standards, had become next to impossible. Train, bus, and airplane schedules were thrown into massive confusion.

They began the journey at the Delhi airport, wondering whether the message sent to their hostess about a change in flights had reached her and whether anyone would be in Allahabad to meet them. If they had any idea of the array of delays and unplanned appointments the next two days would hold, they probably would have scratched the visit from their schedule.

First, the flight was delayed for six hours. As they lunched at the airlines' expense, a young woman from England joined them. She'd been to Allahabad already. Heavy of heart following a recent personal tragedy, she'd mingled among the throngs and listened to the priests passing on wisdom to eager listeners. She'd watched the pilgrims give their alms (special favors resulted from performing charitable acts at a *kumbh mela*) and bathe in the river. She'd begun to wonder whether, after all, there was an essential difference between Hinduism and the Christianity she'd grown up with in England. Lorry and Ethel realized God's purpose in that delay. They reminded this confused searcher of the ways in which Jesus Christ showed Himself to be different. She listened eagerly to all they said and welcomed the Gideon New Testament they offered her.

"I think God must have planned for us to meet," she told them.

Later, on the plane, God gave Ethel a seat next to an American who wore saffron robes, shaved his head, and taught yoga in a city in Southern India. He told her more frankly than any Indian ever did, that he had come here to have his sins washed away. While Lorry prayed, Ethel told him about the power of the blood of Jesus Christ and recounted for him the story of a former Hindu Brahman she had met in Calcutta who used to try to wash his sins away in the river, until Jesus Christ rescued him from such futile routines.

They arrived in Allahabad, a tiny airport located on an Air Force base, late at night, and were met by a young American missionary language student on a motorcycle. Taxis were in short supply. They shared a taxi with the American yoga instructor and followed their motorcyclist friend through the crowded streets of Allahabad.

They stayed the night in an old mission bungalow at a Bible seminary with two missionary ladies whose husbands were out on a trek.

The next day plans changed once more, when they learned that roads were jammed to near impassability going out of the city. They had no time to drive to Shanta's home in Rewa. She hoped to come to where they were, but could not find a driver or a car, since there was a gasoline strike in her town.

Lorry and Ethel spent the morning typing up notes to leave for Shanta. One of the hostesses loaned Ethel her laptop computer, with the same word processing program she used at home. One more touch of God's providence!

Then, since telephones weren't working, they headed back to the airport, just in case their flight might depart on time.

Again, taxis were out of the question, so the language student of the night before found a pair of rickshaws to take them to the travel agency, where they found neither a taxi nor a telephone. They went to the train station. Still no taxi. But their friend found a man with a car, who was waiting to meet a delayed train and offered to take them to the airport.

This time Ethel prayed and Lorry witnessed to a man who seemed open to the gospel presentation and tracts she gave to him. At the airport they learned the plane was three hours late. Airline officials piled them onto a rickety old military bus and took them back to the town they had just come from, for lunch.

To their surprise, when they returned to the airport, they found Shanta waiting with her husband, daughters, and several friends. How they'd managed to get through was amazing. The group had been there for an hour and a half, while Lorry and Ethel lunched downtown. They spent fifteen minutes with the woman they had come thousands of miles to see.

This was too much. In the airplane, Ethel cried out to God in frustration, "I thought You'd sent us here to see Shanta. Why didn't You tell us this was the wrong day to come to Allahabad?"

A parade of faces flashed through Ethel's mind—the woman from England, the yoga instructor from New York, the kind man who'd given them a ride to the airport. "No my child, it was not the wrong day," Ethel seemed to hear God say. "My purpose for this trip was just not quite the same as yours."

"Forgive me, Lord, for complaining," Ethel prayed. "What glories we would have missed had our plans gone through."

Looking Inward: Daily let's become more sensitive to God's purposes for all we do. Let's allow God to replace our complaints over foiled plans with anticipation of what greater glories He has in store.

Looking Outward: God longs for us to stop idolizing our clever plans for efficient ministry and listen to His voice, saying, "This is the way, walk in it...Then He will give the rain for your seed with which you sow the ground, and bread of the increase of the earth; it will be fat and plenteous." (Isaiah 30:21,23) When the best of travel plans yield to the sovereignty of God, His glory shines through.

S.T.O.
Partners International

Forty-one

Saltine
Love, Friendship, and Sacrifice

Vietnam

> Our lives are filled with simple joys
> And blessings without end.
> And one of life's greatest joys
> Is to have a friend. —Author unknown

Hank and Marjorie Jones were in Saigon working with the American chaplains during the Vietnam War. One morning their three children, Ellwood, Dora, and Verda looked out from the fourth floor patio where their bedrooms were located. Dora pointed to the neighbor's yard and exclaimed, "Look! Baby ducks."

Verda immediately chimed in, "I want one. I don't have a pet. I miss the duck we left back home in California."

The three children badgered their parents. Finally their household helper, Nam, bought them two yellow fuzzy baby ducks—in Vietnam you never buy just one. Soon one of the ducklings jumped into a dishpan of gasoline a neighbor had drained from his car. The duck died and its mate grieved for her lost companion.

Dora found a wire cage and named the duck "Saltine" because she was just an ordinary white "quacker." Verda showered the new pet with loving attention, but her grief over leaving her duck family was overwhelming. The kids tried to combat her loneliness but nothing worked. Saltine just wouldn't be friends with them.

At this same time, a hen living in their back yard hatched chicks. Since the chicks were about the same age as Saltine, Nam placed one of the chicks in the cage with the duck. Saltine was overjoyed. The chick, on the other hand, wasn't but tolerated the situation.

When Verda discovered the new roommate, she was upset. The chick was naked. She had lost her baby fuzz, and her feathers were coming in slowly. She had a few scraggly feathers on her tail, wing-tips, and lower legs but nowhere else. In other words, she was bare, hot, and ugly. Saltine was beautiful, soft, warm, and fuzzy.

Verda didn't like the chick so she took her out of the cage. Nam later caught the chick and put her back in. The next morning Verda pulled her out and set the chick in the yard. Nam brought her back. This went on for two days.

Finally Dora said to her sister, "The chicken stays. We're going to hurt Nam's feelings if we don't leave her in the cage." Verda loved Nam and didn't want to upset her so the chicken made her new home in the cage with Saltine.

"What shall we call her?" Dora asked. "We can't just call her 'chicken'."

"How about 'Little Naked' or 'Pure Ugly?'" suggested Verda. The girls giggled.

But gentle thoughtful Dora said, "We better be careful what we name her, because someone may explain to Nam what the chicken's name means."

The children didn't speak any Vietnamese, and Nam didn't speak any English. They communicated by playing charades.

Finally Dora suggested, "Let's call her 'Featherless.'" Verda liked that name, and Featherless shared in all Saltine's activities except swimming.

Each morning the girls carried Saltine and Featherless outside to a small fenced area. They always quarrelled over who would carry Saltine and who had to carry Featherless. Verda hated the feel of the chick's naked flesh.

Because the fence was only about two and a half feet high, Featherless soon learned to fly over the fence to join her natural family in the backyard. At these times, Saltine would pace back and forth along the fence and cry and call. Since all the chicks looked alike, Dora and Verda couldn't tell which one was Featherless. Yet before long, one chick would separate herself from the rest and take the lengthy walk up the driveway. Then more by jumping than flying, Featherless returned to the penned front yard and her lonesome companion.

Saltine had strong wings, but she never tried to fly. Within a week, Featherless no longer left her friend to join her family. It was truly sacrificial love on Featherless's part. She didn't need Saltine. She was happy with her family, but Saltine needed her. Featherless realized this and made the choice to leave her family, her culture, and her language group to be with Saltine.

Featherless's family continued to strut down the driveway at least twice a day to coax her to join them. She wouldn't leave Saltine.

Verda took a coffee can of rice out to Featherless and Saltine every morning. They would come running and eat the rice out of her hand.

Time passed, and Ellwood and Dora went to school in Manila. When Featherless became of marriageable age, Nam thought Verda would enjoy raising baby chicks so she bought a rooster. It didn't appear to be 'love at first sight', but Featherless did accept the rooster's attentions. However, with Saltine it was instant hatred, seasoned with jealousy. She would fly into a rage every time the rooster got near Featherless. The Joneses had to separate the duck and rooster several times a day. Verda began to feel as negatively as Saltine did toward the rooster.

Then one Friday morning, Verda went out to feed her friends. Featherless came. Saltine didn't! Verda looked everywhere she could think of without success. After a couple of hours, she turned the job of hunting over to Nam.

About an hour later, Nam came bounding up the stairs, two and three steps at a time. She had found Saltine in the backyard, lying in an area overgrown with wild rice in the midst of a coil of barbed wire. Almost dead.

Nam helped Verda untangle Saltine and carry her out. She had a broken neck, a broken wing, and a broken leg. Carefully, Verda carried Saltine into the house. Hank brought the wire cage, and they placed the almost lifeless body in a warm area of the kitchen. Featherless stayed by the kitchen door, but she couldn't be coaxed to come in.

Saltine lay flat on her side. By carefully lifting the duck's head, Verda got her to drink a little water, but Saltine would not eat.

With tears streaming down her face Verda asked, "Mother, do you think she'll live?"

Marjorie didn't know how to tell her eleven-year-old daughter that one of her only two playmates was dying. "If she had only a broken wing and a broken leg, then there would be no problem. She would live. She might be crippled, but she'd live. With a broken neck, I don't see how she can survive."

Tears filled Verda's eyes and her lower lip quivered. Marjorie quickly added, "God performed greater miracles than this. All we can do is pray." Because Marjorie had no faith in Saltine's recovery, she didn't pray.

But Verda prayed faithfully for her pet.

Saturday Saltine was still flat on her side with little sign of life. She took a little water, but no food. The rest of the day she lay quietly. Sunday morning Saltine sat on her feet with her neck and head lying on the floor of the cage straight out in front of her. She was in this same position Monday. Verda again asked, "Mother, do you think she'll live?"

Again Marjorie replied, "I don't see how she can."

Tuesday, Saltine raised her head and rested on her back. Marjorie said, "She looks stronger, but she hasn't eaten since last Thursday. Get the rice and see if you can get her to eat."

When Verda approached the cage, Saltine recognized the brightly colored coffee can. Verda put the can down, opened the cage door, and watched.

Saltine hobbled out of the cage. She fell three times before reaching the can, but she made it and ate. Soon she was back outside with her friend, Featherless. They got rid of the rooster once they realized he had attacked Saltine.

A few days later, Verda went out to feed her friends but neither came. She hunted and hunted. After over an hour of searching, Verda, in a whisper, called to her mother, "Come here, I've found them."

Verda led Marjorie back in a dark corner of an old shed. There they heard a soft, "Quack, quack,quack." Then just as softly, "Peep, peep, peep." Featherless was setting on her eggs. Saltine was sitting beside her. They were not only setting on the eggs together, they were visiting!

For twenty-one days the eggs were never alone. If Featherless went for a walk, Saltine stayed with the eggs. If Saltine went, Featherless stayed. Verda carried their food and water to them. Three chicks hatched. Saltine was as proud as Featherless.

In Vietnam, a land whose past was rampant with persecution, poverty, and prejudice, God strengthened this family's understanding of love, friendship, and sacrifice through a little girl, a duck, and a chicken.

Looking Inward: This is a unique story of how God healed a duck simply because a little girl prayed. He chose this method of showing His great love and concern for one American missionary family in

Saigon. He often shows His love for us in seemingly insignificant ways.

Looking Outward: Featherless's sacrifice in leaving her family because a friend needed her is a lesson to us all. Saltine's sacrifice of setting for twenty-one days on eggs that weren't even hers shows true friendship in action. What sacrifices are we willing to make for our friends?

S.T.O.
Spiritual Overseers Service (SOS)

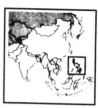

Forty-Two

Eddie Dominguez
Heart for the Headhunters

Philippines

To my God, a heart of flame; to my fellow men, a leart of love; to myself, a heart of steel. —Augustine of Hippo

---

His name was Eddie Dominguez. He had grown up in the tiny Filipino town of Imus, Cavite, in the Luzon Peninsula near Manila. But today he lay dying in a hospital room in Hawaii, awaiting heart surgery. He had suffered with heart trouble since he was a young man, once having undergone a four-and-a-half-hour open heart procedure back in the Philippines.

Many strenuous years of Eddie's life, spent in tribal work in remote villages of the island country, had further weakened his heart and forced him to give up his village ministry. He then became a teacher in the Philippine Missionary Institute, where he could be near medical help.

Yet, those who remembered Eddie Dominguez and saw his ministry over the years would have said there was nothing wrong with Eddie's heart—at least, not the heart God put in him—the heart that beat for the tribal people of his island country.

Eddie had grown up as any other young Filipino boy of his village on the Luzon peninsula. His sister made sure he attended Sunday school, but after church he would join his friends to watch the cock fights or to serenade some pretty young village girl, or whatever else sounded exciting.

Eddie's older brother Arsenio had become a Christian and was attending a nearby Bible college started by some American military men after World War II. Arsenio became concerned about his little brother and brought him some good books to read.

Eddie was impressed by the changes he saw in his brother, and soon Arsenio was able to lead Eddie to Christ. Later Arsenio gave him a little book from the Moody Colportage Library, *Thinking with God*, which challenged him to commit his life fully to Christ. In a few years Eddie had followed his brother to Bible college to begin studying. He turned out to be an excellent student as well as a hard worker to pay for his schooling.

Again, following Arsenio's example, Eddie began to pray about missionary work among the tribal people scattered through the interior of the islands. After graduation he married his childhood sweetheart, Lydia, a girl whose mother had died in childbirth. Lydia was cared for by the head nurse of the hospital who raised her as her own daughter.

Just as they entered missionary training, a doctor who happened to be treating Lydia noticed how exhausted Eddie was becoming and sent him to see a heart specialist. It was then that they learned that his heart problem was serious and needed immediate surgery.

Eddie's recovery from the four-hour ordeal on the operating table was remarkable, giving him a new lease on life. Soon he and Lydia began their work in a remote section of the islands, trying to reach a tribe called the Ilongots. When the young couple first arrived among the Ilongots, they were greeted with suspicion. This tribe was one of the most vicious in the area. Mostly nomadic, they roamed the countryside, hunting deer, wild pigs, and human heads. A group of tribesmen had just made a sweep through a nearby lowland village, killing thirteen people. The tribesman suspected that Eddie had been sent by the constabulary to spy on them.

One dark night a group of tribesmen surrounded the hut where Eddie and Lydia were staying, intent on killing them. Years later they explained why they didn't carry out their plan. They said a bright light shone from the hut, blinding them, causing them to fall noisily, and making them flee in confusion. Eddie and Lydia slept on, never knowing they were ever in any danger.

Later another light shone out in the village. As the truth of the gospel spread, many of the Ilongots came to know Christ. One later said, "The Lord must surely have prevented us from killing you because He intends that you be our brother and sister through faith in Christ."

When the Ilongots asked where the light had come from, Eddie read them the verse, "The angel of the Lord encamps all around those who fear Him, and delivers them" (Psalm 34:7).

How different it was years later, when on another dark night Lydia was stricken with an attack of malaria! Waking up to take her medicine, she heard noises. Their pet monkey began screaming. She woke her husband, who took a light and went to see what was causing the racket.

"Get up and call for help," he said. "It's the largest snake I've ever seen. He has already coated the monkey with saliva, trying to swallow him."

This time the Ilongot villagers came, not to kill them, but as friends to protect them. What a difference the light of the gospel had made!

Later, when Eddie's heart condition worsened, his son knew to survive he would need a coronary by-pass operation, so he had taken his father to Hawaii for the surgery. Eddie died before the surgery could be performed. His last words to his son Nathaniel were "I love you, son."

Eddie's physical heart, weak as it was, was not slowed from what he called "a cause big enough and noble enough" to motivate him all the days of his life. As he wrote, some years before his death, "There are many other tribes still waiting for the light of the gospel to shine in their hearts and lives."

Looking Inward: All of us live for something or someone—our hearts beat strongly, passionately, for those things we consider most important. If God were to search our hearts today, to see the things for which our hearts beat today, what would he find?

Looking Outward: All we have, our money, our talents, and our physical strength, are ours not as ownership but as stewardship. Eddie Dominguez must have known that, using all he had for all God had for him to do. May our hearts, like Eddie's, beat for those things most precious to the heart of God—the lost of the world.

W.W.
SEND International

Forty-three

Stephanie
The Street Orphan

Korea

We receive more than we can ever give; we receive it from the past on which we draw with each breath, but also—and this is a point of faith—from the source of the mystery itself, by the means which religious people call *grace*. —Edwin Muir

---

She was born in Korea, right after the war that nearly destroyed that country and left thousands of orphaned and mix-blooded children like her, fathered by a foreign soldier. Everyone was so poor that children of mixed blood were often put to death by the midwives.

She was different, because somehow she lived. Her mother must have loved her and tried to take care of her, but being poor, she had to abandon the child in the streets as were so many others youths.

For about seven years she roamed the streets with other orphans, eating mice, grasshoppers, locusts, and grass. They lived in caves, under bridges. Everyday she saw other children die all around her. When they wandered into towns or villages, the people screamed at them, calling g them an insulting name, "child of two bloods." She was dirty and looked hardly human. She wasn't a Korean, had no name, and no hope of ever getting a job or getting married.

Once some men caught her—she couldn't remember why, but she had probably stolen from them. They threw her and another girl into a building infested with rats as big as cats, mean and vicious. If the rats were hungry they attacked anything in their sight. The rats attacked the other girl, but somehow she survived.

A wave of cholera swept Korea, and as a weakened street child, she became ill. At that stage, she would have welcomed death, having suffered so long, and with no future. About that time World Vision sent workers into the streets, instructed to pick up only infants and children under three because they simply didn't have room for everyone. One of the World Vision nurse, Iris Erickson, found her lying in the street, nearly dead, and decided to take her back to the orphanage with her. The Lord somehow told Iris that he had a purpose for that child. At first the nurse argued with God, but in the end she decided to take the child to her home where she nursed her back to life.

When the little girl was strong enough, the nurse found her a place in a World Vision orphanage, where she was given a job of washing out cloth diapers. Laundry was done down by the river, where they beat the clothes out with a big stick. She didn't mind, because for the first time she had a roof over her head, three good meals a day, and people who cared about her.

There in the orphanage, she also learned for the first time that she could give love, the way she had received it. The little babies in the orphanage were so tiny and helpless, and the workers were so busy they had little time to spend with each child. She spent hours holding little ones in her arms and loving them.

One day she learned that some foreigners were coming to the orphanage, and that they might choose one of the children to take to their home. She got busy scrubbing babies and putting ribbons in their hair to make them look as nice as possible.

Finally the foreign couple arrived. She had remembered hearing Bible stories about the giant Goliath, and when the man arrived, she thought Goliath must be alive again. At first she was afraid of him, because all grown men she had known had mistreated her, like the ones who threw her into the rat-infested building. But this man was different. She could see compassion in his face. Tears ran down his cheek as he picked up the little babies, one after another. Then suddenly he turned towards her.

At the time she was almost nine years old, but weighed less than thirty pounds. She was scrawny, had boils all over her skin and scars all over my body. She knew she was not a pretty sight.

But that huge man took his hand and laid it on her face. It seemed to cover not only her face but half her scrawny body. It felt so good! Inside she was begging, *"Oh, keep it up—don't let go."*

That is what she said inside. But reacting to her past experience with men, she jerked away and spit on him. The man and his wife turned to leave.

The next day she knew there must be a God and that he worked miracles. The man and his wife returned and took her home with them, even after she had spit on him!

For the first time she knew what a bed was. Her new parents bought dresses for her, and by adoption, she became an American citizen. And, for the first time she was given a name, Stephanie. They were very good to her, but her past had taken a toll on her emotionally.

One day when Stephanie was fifteen, her father came into the room and began to tell her about Jesus, who also had a very bad start, humanly speaking. "Think about Jesus," he told her. "He was born in a stinking stable. He went to his home town and was rejected by friends and relatives. Even his disciples deserted him when he was arrested."

Then he began to explain what Jesus could do for her. "You have been hurt—despised, rejected, and abused. But Jesus went through all that too, so he knows all about you."

Later Stephanie said, "Since the day I was thrown into the building with the rats, I hadn't cried a tear, but in my room that night the Lord released my emotions, and I began to cry. That was the night the healing began."

Since that time, Stephanie has married and raised a family. She and her husband have served as missionaries, and later worked at a Christian academy in British Columbia.

God's plan is perfect. Through years of living in the streets as an orphan child, eating locusts and grasshoppers, and all manner of sickness, God's plan was unfolding. His loving hand—much bigger than the huge hand of her father, or Goliath—was placed on her. Through the love of a nurse who was struggling against her own urges to leave the child there and choose younger children who had a better chance to live, God picked her up. A nameless child, left to die on the street, was picked up by a God of love and put on the road that led to physical, emotional, and spiritual health.

Looking Inward: We have probably never been reduced to eating locusts and grasshoppers; nor have we ever been left on the streets to die. But we must never forget that we were just as hopeless until God's mercy reached down to us.

Looking Outward: We pass many needy people every day—some may be well dressed, but overwhelmed by life's problems and dying with no hope. Others languish in poverty and disease. Jesus said, "Inasmuch as you did it to one of the least of these My brethren, you did it to Me" (Matthew 25:40).

S.T.O.
World Vision

Forty-Four

Baba Lehin
A Price to Pay

Nigeria

I have decided to follow Jesus,
I have decided to follow Jesus,
I have decided to follow Jesus,
No turning back! No turning back! —folk melody of India

He knew his life had been changed, but little did he know how much—and how much it would affect him. Each week Baba Lehim walked about ten miles out of the thick forest to meet with his friend, Tommy Titcombe, who came to hold a Bible study and reading class with him and several other young men who had received Christ. The Bible lessons were simple, but filled with life-changing truths. The reading lessons were coming slowly, but soon he was able to understand several verses from the Bible for himself.

Each time he walked past the circle of posts where the devil worship rituals were being practiced, he got either laughter or insults from the older men who gathered there. At night, as he passed the ring of shiny human skulls, mounted on top of each of the posts, they gave off eerie reflections from the fire burning in the center. The hollow eyes of the skeletons seemed to be watching him as he passed.

He didn't go to that circle with the other men anymore since he had received Jesus into his life. But he still had the malevolent feelings each time he passed the ju-ju shrine. From his tiny hut on the edge of the village, he could see the bonfires and hear the loud chantings and screams coming from the devil worshippers.

Before the sounds had filled him with excitement, but now, understanding better the nature of a holy God and the nature of evil spirits in the world, he felt a deep sadness inside for his people.

More and more he could feel the angry eyes of the older men on him as he went about his work. Then he heard that the village elders had passed the word around that no one from that town was to give him a wife when the time came for marriage. When it was time to replace the thatch on the roofs of the huts, it was common courtesy for your neighbors and friends to stand on the ground and toss up bundles of straw to the person sitting on the roof, thatching the long tough grasses in place to form a watertight covering. No one would toss straw for him, which meant he climbed up and down a rickety make-shift ladder for each of the many bundles of straw needed to repair his roof. In every way he was treated like an outcast, and there was not one other believer in the village who would sympathize with him or help him.

Some time later ugly sores broke out on his legs, and he suspected someone in the village was poisoning him. Several times he felt nauseated after eating his evening meal, but he eventually recovered. Then he began to notice the little piles of poison someone was leaving around in his hut, and he often found strange amulets, ju-ju curses, hanging around his hut. It was clear the old men were trying to kill him.

Although fearful, he didn't give up and leave his village. Instead, he prayed, and asked his Christian friends with whom he met weekly for Bible study to pray also.

Then one day some of the men came to have a talk with him. They asked him about his new faith, why he didn't worship their gods at their ju-ju shrine anymore, and where he was getting his "power." Then they confessed that they had tried every way they knew to kill him, but their "medicine" wasn't working against him. They reasoned that his God had given him some cure that they didn't know about, so they had come to know more about what had broken their powers.

Whether the young man knew the verse was in the Bible or not, God was being faithful to His Word given through Moses: "No man shall be able to stand against you; the Lord your God will put the fear of you upon on all the land where you tread, just as He has said to you (Deuteronomy 11:25).

That was many years ago. A vibrant church stands in that remote village today. Beside the church is a cement-capped tomb, the kind only placed on unusually important graves. It is the tomb of Baba Lehim, the first believer, who became also the first pastor in that village. The ju-ju shrine was torn down many years ago. Only a few older people even remember where it stood. The village is still primitive—no motor roads leading into town, no electricity or running water, no government buildings or post office. Since it is so far from the main roads, it may never become a large town. In years to come, they may even forget what took place there. But sometimes late at night, sitting around flickering fires, the old people occasionally tell about the young man, and how nobody would throw straw for him. And they tell their young boys about how this young man prayed to his God and broke the dark power in that village.

Looking Inward: When the truth breaks through to our hearts, we must change the way we live, or else we begin to live a lie. Sometimes standing for the truth will cost us something—but the price of maintaining our integrity before God has its own rewards.

Looking Outward: Unless we live up to the truth —no matter what it may cost us—others will never find the truth for themselves. We may never face the outward persecutions, the unfriendliness, even the poison of others, but there will be a price to pay. Yet, the reward of seeing God's harvest makes the cost seem worthwhile.

W. W.
SIM International

Forty-Five

Condemned by Man
But Loved by God

USA

Some want to live within the sound of church and chapel bell: I want to run a rescue ship within a yard of hell! —C.T. Studd

---

Rodney Brown was the first to step forward. Chaplains Janalee and Gary Hoffman had requested to see him alone. The guards were supposed to return him to his death row cell before the other inmates arrived, but they left Rodney behind. He had made a lot of enemies with his bullying tactics, and some of the men were uncomfortable with his presence in the room. They were afraid Rodney would "go off."

Rodney had witnessed the murder of his mother when he was three years old and was raised by his abusive father. His tour of military duty in Vietnam did further damage to the broken child who had grown into an angry adult. Years of drug and alcohol abuse were a mask to hide the pain Rodney felt inside. The other prisoners watched guardedly, as much to protect the Hoffmans as each other.

Gary had spent a considerable amount of time talking to Rodney before the others arrived. "Rodney," Gary said, "you have to walk that walk if you are going to talk that talk. It costs nothing to become a Christian, but it costs everything to live the Christian life. Jesus said we are to count the cost if we are to be His followers. You had better get out your calculator."

Now in front of his peers, Rodney cleared his throat nervously as his eyes scanned each face. "I have hurt many of you with my past actions and attitudes. I'm sorry for all I've done, and I ask your forgiveness. I promise I will try to do better in the future. I don't know if I'll be successful, but I promise I'll try my best with Jesus' help. I know if I claim to be a Christian, I must live like one, and I haven't done a very good job of it. I would like to be baptized with you today."

Gary held the silver dish as Janalee poured the water. She said, "I baptize you, Rodney, in the name of the Father, and of the Son, and of the Holy Spirit. Amen."

Some of the prisoners were deeply moved by what Rodney said. Others thought it was just a con. He'd caused a lot of hurt in the past. Another prisoner who wasn't a Christian yet said to Janalee later, "Jan, whether Rodney can live what he preached is yet to be proven, but I believe he sincerely meant every word he spoke at that moment. I'm willing to give him a chance."

The inmate photographer took pictures and listened intently as each of the eleven men came forward to be baptized.

Sandy Davis brought tears to almost everyone's eyes when he said, "I served Satan when I was out on the streets. We all serve him in one way or another unless we consciously make a decision to serve Christ, but I chose to worship Satan. Today is Good Friday, the day Jesus gave His life for each of us. It is the day I choose to publicly and proudly give my life back to Him."

As a young child, Sandy had been taken to a variety of churches by his mother. On three occasions, Sandy had asked the ministers questions after the services. He was told by each that he would go to hell for asking such questions. In his teen years, Sandy turned to satanism because he thought God hated him. He decided the best deal he could make for himself was with the devil. Sandy was arrested for first degree murder at the age of nineteen and sentenced to death.

While he was waiting trial in the county jail, another prisoner asked Sandy if he would go to a Bible Study in the Chapel. Sandy said, "Yes," to escape the noise of the unit. The chaplain lovingly explained to Sandy that God didn't hate him, but rather He loved him so much that He sent His Son, Jesus, to die for his sins. All that night, Sandy lay awake thinking about what the chaplain had told him. The next night, Sandy went back to the Chapel and prayed for Jesus to come into his heart.

Janalee looked around the room. It contained both Christians and non-believers. As her eyes scanned each face, they locked on Johnny Fry. He squirmed in his chair. She said, Johnny, are you ready to be baptized?"

154

Johnny's face turned pink as he shook his snow white hair and said, "Not yet, maybe next time."

Johnny had been convicted of murdering a prostitute. He had been on death row longer than any one else in the state. He was private and reserved regarding his faith. Perhaps next time he would be ready.

Shortly after the baptisms ended, the guards came to claim their captives. Although everyone groaned and no one wanted the visit to end, each death row inmate needed time alone to reflect on what had happened that day. No one walked away from that room unaffected.

The Hoffmans returned to their home in Las Vegas and began editing the next issue of *The Rising Son,* their ministry's magazine that is written by and distributed to death row inmates. Sandy Davis sent the following article to be included:

Making the decision to be baptized was one of the most important decisions I've ever made. Not just for the obvious reasons, but because of my past involvement with witchcraft and the occult. Baptism is a serious matter to me. I believe it should be a conscious decision with a lot of thought for its meaning. Jesus instructed us to count the cost before we commit our lives to Him.

I was baptized April 16th, 1987, shortly after my 22nd birthday. I had to decide between the constant temptations of practicing witchcraft again or putting it all behind me and doing the very best I could to serve God. I didn't want to be baptized until I could make a commitment to Christ to serve Him with my whole heart, mind, and soul.

It was not only a commitment to God and to myself, but a way of letting God know I had made a decision to turn away from witchcraft and all its evils to serve Him to the best of my ability. It was a public declaration of my love for Him. I want to be what He wants me to be, and I want Him to guide my life in whatever direction He wants.

Jan and Gary came to the prison on Good Friday and baptized eleven of us men. They made me feel comfortable. I was nervous, not because everyone else was there, but because of how important the event was in my life. It was even more special to me because they were the ones to baptize me. Good Friday was the day Jesus laid down His life so we could live, and it is the day we publicly gave our lives back to Him.

It took a lot of courage for those men on death row to stand before their non-believing peers and take the stand they did. When Jan recalls April 16, 1987, she thinks of Isaiah 49:16: "See, I have inscribed you on the palms of My hands."

Many people doubt what they call "jailhouse conversions." They think that men and women in prison use "religion" as a way out the back door. At times there are some in prison who use it as a con. They get Christians from the community to write letters to the parole board on their behalf, and they ask these Christians to help them find jobs.

However, there is nothing material for a death row inmate to gain by professing to be a Christian. These prisoners never go before a parole board.

Looking Inward: Perhaps we, too, should take a moment to count the cost of our commitment to Jesus Christ. Let's try to be all that He wants us to be and do all that He wants us to do. Let's renew our commitment to Him by saying, "Here I am, Lord. Use me."

Looking Outward: On Good Friday, Jesus publicly gave His life for each of us. On Good Friday, eleven death row men were willing to be baptized and suffer persecution from other inmates. How are we willing to show our faith and love for our Savior?

S.T.O.
The Rising Son Ministries

Forty-six

From Headhunter
To Hallelujah Choir

India

We do the works, but God works in us the doing of the works. —St. Augustine of Hippo

---

Amy's dream since she was a little girl was to become a missionary doctor. Her high school teachers thought she would pass the necessary exams required in India for a student to take up scientific fields, but she didn't score high enough.

In her disappointment, she cried, "Lord I'm trying to serve you. What are you doing? I'd rather die than not serve you."

However after Amy completed her two-year degree course, she was asked to teach in a new Christian private school in Arunachal. The pioneers who started the school had a vision of bringing in children from the pagan neighboring province where outsiders were not allowed to enter. The main intention of the school was to train these children so that they could return to their villages, bringing the gospel of Jesus Christ to their friends and family members.

Amy accepted the invitation to teach at the new Christian school—a school which had many problems when it first opened. Many of the young children missed their parents, and they cried themselves to sleep at night. Some needed diapers. Many developed prickly heat. They had no electricity—only lanterns. But Amy and the other teachers learned to comfort and to manage thirty-three small children ranging in age from four to six.

In time, the children learned to love one another, to pray for one another, and to cheer up one another. Ninety percent accepted Christ. The rest were too young to make that commitment. The young students were an inspiration to their parents, and some of them accepted Christ, too.

One student who stands out in Amy's mind was Prem. When Prem first came to the school, he was dirty, unruly, and streetwise. Prem became the hero of the school. He was also bright and picked up the Word of God quickly. One morning during devotions, he listened to Matthew 5:39. "But I tell you not to resist an evil person. But whoever slaps you on your right cheek, turn the other to him also."

Later that afternoon, another boy tried to pick a fight with Prem and hit him in the face, but Prem turned the other cheek. The other boy was so surprised that he walked away.

Prem came to Amy and said, "Madam, what you said this morning was true. Mari hit me, and I offered him my other cheek."

Amy laughed with her young friend. Was this the same boy who used to steal his parents coins? Prem used to sneak into movie houses without paying. He would try to cheat people drunk with wine. Now he had left his street life far behind.

Amy felt blessed when she saw results in the children such as the change in Prem. She believed the children really understood the gospel. Sometimes it seemed they showed more faith than she did. Their faith was compacted and undiluted—so pure and beautiful.

Amy thought of her students and then recalled the day she had never wanted to become a teacher. Her heart had been set on becoming a missionary doctor. When first offered the teaching position she had said, "Lord, this is not where I want to go."

But now she realized that God had other plans for her. And her young students taught her as much as she taught them.

One student named Dedo was sick with malaria. Amy prayed with him, but he didn't get better. One evening she went to his bedroom to pray with him again.

"She asked, "Dedo, how do you feel."

He answered, "I'm not very well."

Amy asked, "Are you angry with God?"

He replied, "No, Madam. You told me everything I've got is from God, whether good or bad. If this is from God, it is fine with me. I just praise God however I am."

What an example of faith Amy saw in this student. She always trusted Dedo after that, and he became her favorite student. He also became a leader, and eventually his family was the first to convert to Christianity. Sickness such as this was a blessing because it taught the children how to pray, and that God answers prayer.

Before leaving the school to continue her education in America Amy told Dedo, "I am counting on you to finish the work in Arunachal."

He said, "Madam, I'll do it."

She replied, "It won't be easy. You might be persecuted. You might be thrown out of your home and have to go without food. You might have to die for Christianity. What would you say to that?"

"It's all right, Madam. God loves me so much, I'm going to do it."

Amy looked toward the mountains that separated the two provinces.

Her student continued, "We will go, we will fight, and we will win. This is our land. Don't worry, we will complete the work you have started."

Amy comes from the small state of Misoram from a tribe that were once head-hunters. Presbyterian missionaries from Wales originally brought the gospel to them. Today ninety-five percent of the Miso people are Christians. They say they are involved in evangelism because the first Christians who evangelized them came from far away. They were blessed by a far country, so they reach out to far countries as well as their own nation of India whose population contains only four percent Christians.

Just as these children are getting an education so they can evangelize their villages, Amy is now at the Grand Rapids School of the Bible. She is majoring in missions. Perhaps one day she will return to her own country as a missionary doctor—not a medical doctor, but a doctor of theology. Then she can continue lighting a fire within her own people to strengthen their faith.

Looking Inward: Amy's grandfather once told her, "You must be your best for God." God expects our best from us, too. But first we must be in tune with Him so we can know His will for our lives. Then, when we know His will, we must be willing to do whatever He asks of us.

Looking Outnward: Sometimes we think we know what God has in mind for us without prayerfully asking Him. Yet, God's plans for us often turn out to be different than we imagined. Like Amy, we, too, need to learn to live one day at a time staying in tune with God's will for our lives. The results may be rewards greater than ever imagined.

S.T.O.
Christian Missions in Many Lands

Forty-seven

Ah-Mei and
The Peach Tree

China

To walk in the light requires us to accept our responsibilities
without reserve, to own our sin that we may be able to disown
it. . . . The man who has a guilty secret in his life is a lonely
man. . . . The cleansing virtue of the atonement cannot reach
him where he dwells by himself in the dark. —James Denney,
from *The Way Everlasting*

The village doctor seemed troubled as he wrapped the dried
herbs in brown paper and handed the packet to the distraught
woman.

"It is indeed strange that your daughter has not recovered,"
he told Ah-Mei's mother. "Everything else has failed, but perhaps
this will cure little sister's illness."

Everyone seemed to know everybody else in their small village
in Yunnan Province of southern China. All the people knew about
little Ah-Mei and her strange illness. Most of the people were
Christians. Many of them climbed the steep pathways to the
family's hut to pray for the twelve-year-old girl, who was having
a hard time digesting food. She seemed to grow weaker each day.

When spring came, the family in desperation made the long
journey with the child to the government clinic for treatment.
There they were given the news that they didn't know how to
treat her problem. Filled with discouragement, the long journey
home seemed even longer. In spite of the family's sadness, Ah-
Mei's spirit remained bright. She loved to sing with the Christians,
and often she was heard singing to herself in the corner of the hut.

Soon the little girl became so weak she lay on her mat, unable to speak or move. News spread through the village, and a group of Christians met at her home to pray. Why did God not heal her daughter? Ah-Mei's mother prayed, more fervently than ever.

Then without a sound, the little girl stopped breathing. Was she gone? "It can't be!" one of them said, and they continued to pray. Another hour passed. Suddenly the girl's mother concluded the prayer with a firm, "Amen!"

Suddenly her daughter's eyes opened, and she sat upright. "Did you see Him? He was just here! I saw the Lord Jesus! He was standing here beside me!"

"Did He speak?" one of the women asked, her voice filled with awe.

"He said I would be well! Jesus will heal me . . . but not yet! When the peaches are ripe," he said. With that, the little girl lay back again.

Why had God allowed this to happen? There must be a reason, they thought. Then Grandmother Wang, the oldest woman in the room, sensed there was more they should know. "What else did he say?" she asked.

Ah-Mei, pulling her strength together, gave them the rest of the message. It was about sin problems in their church. It seemed that God wanted to use this occasion, when all these people were before Him in humility, to tell them what they weren't willing to hear in any other way.

"He wants everyone to repent," she began. She recounted that Jesus had talked to her about all the lukewarm Christians in the village who didn't really trust Him completely. She told about an elder's family and the discord in the home, about children who were angry with each other, about a daughter who sang in the choir but wouldn't speak or even eat with her brother and sister-in-law. Weak and exhausted after giving her divine message, Ah-Mei slumped back onto the mat.

The sound of soft sobbing filled the room. It was the elder's daughter, crying out her prayer to God for forgiveness. It was a beginning—a springtime of faith and renewal—the budding of new life in their church, like the swelling buds on the peach trees nearby.

God has given us His Word: "Is anyone among you suffering? Let him pray. . . . And the prayer of faith will save the sick. . . . And if he has committed sins, he will be forgiven" (James 5:13-15).

Two months passed, and Ah-Mei grew stronger each day. Putting on her wide bodice and beautiful flowered skirt, she joined the village women, all dressed in the same fashion, in a joyful procession. It was Ah-Mei's day. The women sang as they walked solemnly to the peach orchards. The peaches were ripe. The little girl was well. And many hearts were healed.

Looking Inward: Sometimes God has to get our attention by touching our bodies. Yet, He never sends trouble or sickness to mock us, but to show us how powerful He is to heal us if He chooses. Or how much grace He can give us to endure.

Looking Outward: What God does for us—whether it be pain or pleasure—He often has others in mind whom He wants to touch. Our hearts must always be willing to allow God to use us in any way he chooses—by life or by death.

S.T.O.
Asian Outreach

Forty-eight

Mrs. Wu
And the Chipped Idol

China

Your eagerness to mortify yourself should never turn you
from solitude, nor tear you away from external affairs. You
must show yourself and hide yourself in turn, and speak and
be still. God has not placed you under a bushel, but on a
candlestick, so that you may light all those who are in the house.
—Fenelon, from *Christian Perfection*

Mrs. Wu missed her nice home in the city. During the Cultural
Revolution, her family was forced to move far away to a rural
area and made to do heavy farm work. Now she was ill and
growing worse, but to avoid ridicule, she continued to work. The
local doctor had offered no help—in fact, she seemed to be worse.
Her family was faced with a decision.

Red candles flickered on the wall shelf which served as a
Buddhist shrine. Behind the candles a god with a fierce looking
painted face glared down on them, seemingly unappeased by the
incense offered to him.

All forms of worship had been banned by the government.
The local Communist Party cadre, who passed the house often,
thought they could smell incense inside. Because the Wu family
had been sent to the country for political reasons, the cadre thought
they needed a special watch placed on them, but their worship
habits, though illegal, were not a primary concern.

Mr. Wu finally spoke. "We must go to the city for help. Elder
Daughter will go with us to care for Mother." Mr. Wu looked

uneasily at the scowling face of the poster on the god shelf. He wondered if they were making the right decision.

Hopes fell when the doctor in the city gave an even more discouraging report. Mrs. Wu would not get better without surgery, and it looked like her worsened heart condition would make surgery inadvisable.

With all other hope gone, Mrs. Wu remembered the old temple where she used to worship. By then, with the Cultural Revolution underway, the temple was being used as a warehouse, but the family went there anyway. Groping around in the darkened building, Mrs. Wu found the old Buddhist idol, now dusty and battered. Looking at the bulging eyes and the fearsome face brought back many memories. She knelt with her head touching the floor and offered her petition. But how could a chipped, dusty idol, now shoved into a dark corner, help?

Mrs. Wu thought that as long as she was in the city, they should try to look up some of her old friends. Approaching a friend's home, she was surprised to hear singing. Inside, her friend greeted her warmly and offered tea to her, Mr. Wu, and their daughter.

The singing continued. "What does this all mean?" Mrs. Wu asked. She listened as the speaker mentioned the name Jesus several times, someone who was present but unseen, yet could hear their prayers.

"How can you worship a god you cannot see?" she asked.

After the meeting, the Christians gathered around and with great simplicity they explained who Jesus was. Then they stood around Mrs. Wu and prayed in Jesus' name that she would be healed.

They taught Mrs. Wu to pray the simple prayer, "Lord, save me," which she prayed over and over.

The next morning when she awoke, she felt hungry, a remarkable change, so remarkable that she and her daughter returned to her friend's house to learn more. "How had it happened? How can we know Jesus?"

Her friend opened the Scriptures, and Mrs. Wu heard more about Jesus. Faith and hope filled her heart as she returned with her family back to their home in the country.

Mrs. Wu's health became gradually stronger, but her faith was still weak. Yet God, in his goodness, met the needs of her growing faith. On several occasions she awoke to find whiteclad spirit beings around her bed, and finally one who assured her that Jesus would heal her completely. From that moment on every trace of the swelling, pain, and weakness was gone from her body.

The local Communist Party cadre who continued to pass the house, became curious that he no longer smelled the incense. Word then came to him at the local teahouse that the Wu family's Buddhist shrine was gone. "I must learn about this," he said, and came to visit the Wu family to see for himself. What he found was another kind of incense pervading the house, the aura of Jesus, who had come to take the place of fearsome looking worship posters. The light of God's Word replaced the flickering candles on the shelf.

Jesus said, "As long as I am in the world, I am the light of the world" (John 9:5).

Soon others in the village were coming to "the light," as Mrs. Wu shared with them what Jesus had done in healing her. At the invitation of the Wu family, Christians began visiting from the city, and soon many others became baptized believers—even the curious cadre man.

Looking Inward: Jesus may not heal our physical bodies or send angels to appear to us. But He knows our needs, and what it takes to strengthen our faith.

Looking Outward: God's work in our lives is rarely for us alone. As His healing comes into our lives, along with it comes the grace that healed us. We are to able to pass this on to others who need healing for their souls.

W.W.
Asian Outreach

Forty-nine

Lester
A Harvest in the Desert

Jordan

In all our spiritual dryness and barrennesses let us never lose courage but, waiting with patience for the return of consolation, earnestly pursue our course.... It is no great matter to serve a prince in the quietness of a time of peace and amongst the delights of the court; but to serve him amidst the hardships of war, in troubles and persecutions, is a true mark of constancy and fidelity. Francis de Sales, from *Introduction to the Devout Life*

The desert land of Jordan, where the Samaritan's Purse volunteers labored to build a hospital for the local Bedouin people, was especially dry and hot. Rainfall was sparse—almost nonexistent sometimes.

All day Franklin Graham, then a college student working on the hospital project, labored in the hot desert sun. He watched the Bedouin people passing by, looking on with curiosity, but not stopping. It was hard to find a means of talking with them.

Apart from their few flocks, they had little to subsist on other than a few crops they grubbed out of the ground if and when rain did fall.

Lester, one of the men permanently stationed there, kept watching and praying, trying to think of a way to reach the Bedouins he saw every day.

There are some things one doesn't expect in the desert—one is steady rains. The other, in the desert lands of the Middle East, is the steady rain of God's Word falling on the parched, arid soil of the hearts of these desert people. Many of them for centuries have been steeped in the teachings of Islam.

Lester kept praying. One day, he decided to act.

Franklin was surprised when Lester told him what he planned to do. The next day, working on the hospital roof, he watched Lester begin preparing a plot of ground which he sowed in wheat. Franklin felt a wave of sadness, thinking that Lester was sure to fail—no wheat was going to germinate in that dry soil. Franklin went to bed feeling sad that night. Here Lester was, praying and hoping for a harvest, and Franklin hated to see him disappointed.

At night the dry desert air cooled off. The most comfortable place to sleep was outdoors—on the roof of the hospital still under construction.

But that night Franklin was awakened. Something had fallen on his face—a drop of water. Then another. It was rain! Before long a steady shower was soaking the earth and his bedding. He jumped and ran for cover.

A few weeks later, from the hospital roof, Franklin watched Lester standing by his field of bright green wheat. Surrounding him was a group of Bedouin farmers, talking excitedly.

It was a breakthrough. Unexpected, but all the same a real breakthrough. It was the kind of opening that only God could make, as the time years later when the rains of God's Word fell on other desert soil, as thousands of believers, American soldiers, entered the desert lands of Saudi Arabia and surrounding countries. Despite the concern of Islamic governments, the gospel was daily being spread, as uncontrollably as falling rain.

God promised his people, speaking of the time when Christ's blessings would reach the entire world, that "He will make her wilderness like Eden, and her desert like the garden of the Lord; joy and gladness will be found in it, thanksgiving and the voice of melody" (Isaiah 51:3).

Franklin's organization, Samaritan's Purse, began shipping literature to the servicemen, who in turn were discreetly distributing it to men in the area. Even Iraqi prisoners of war were soon hearing the gospel for the first time as the faithful rain of God's Word fell softly, causing the seed of the Word to sprout and bring forth a harvest in the hearts of desert people.

Looking Inward: In the dryness of our own hearts, we fail to see what God can do. When we plant in hope, waiting for God's time, he can bring freshness to our souls.

Looking Outward: We live in a world of desert. We are called, despite what the soil looks like, to be faithful in planting the seed of God's Word. Our job is not to produce the rain that causes the seed to sprout—that is God's part. Our part is to sow in faith and wait for the harvest to come.

Samaritan's Purse
W.W.

Fifty

Elijah
From Ashes to Hope

Kenya

God has a thousand ways where I can see not one,
When all my means have reached their end,
Then His have just begun. - Esther Guyot

Pastor Elijah Yano wiped his face with the rag he used as a handkerchief. Carefully folding it, he replaced it in his back pocket. Then shielding his eyes, he squinted at the desert sun to determine the time. He had been hiking the steep escarpment trails all afternoon, visiting members of one of his small congregations. Briefly he gazed over the patchwork of parched farm plots that quilted the valley floor. The harvest of millet and corn would be marginal again this year. There would be hunger in his congregations.

For a young man, Elijah had tremendous responsibilities. Five small churches in the Kerio Valley in Kenya depended on him for spiritual leadership. He served as secretary to the Church Council, helped plan youth camps, and witnessed regularly during local markets along the valley floor.

He turned downhill and quickened his pace. Despite the heat, he soon trotted briskly toward the valley floor to meet some young people to plan a day of witnessing in the market the next morning. Elijah wanted the youth to sing several songs to help attract people to hear him speak. Almost all the members of his language group practiced the traditional religion of their ancestors.

As Elijah ran down the steep, rocky trails with the sure, grace of the small deer-like dikers he sometimes hunted, his mind was on the message he would preach the next day. He couldn't quite remember what he'd learned about the passage he wanted to use. He'd have to search in some of the textbooks he'd saved from Bible school. Most of them were in English, but he knew how fortunate he was to own them.

His English was halting, but his Swahili was quite good. Despite three years of formal training at Bible school, he had difficulty understanding the Bible. Endo, his mother tongue, had only recently been analyzed. Although an alphabet had been approved and was being tested, there were no books available in the language he understood best.

Through the years, Elijah had accumulated over thirty precious volumes in English and Swahili. He kept these in a small wooden bookcase he had built. The base of the bookcase sat on tin cans hammered flat to keep the wood off the hard-packed dirt floor of his grass-roofed hut. The case also sat slightly away from the mud-plastered walls. Otherwise, white ants would quickly have destroyed the library. He frequently removed each book from the shelves to shake out crickets that ate glue from the spines. While a book was out, he would carefully wipe away the droppings left by small geckos.

Barely breathing hard despite the brisk two mile jog, he reached the small church and walked to the shaded side. To his disappointment, none of the young people he expected were waiting outside the metal-roofed, mud building. Taking a small key from his pocket, he unlocked the brass lock, opened the peeling blue-painted door, and slipped into the shady interior. He walked to the front and straightened the embroidered cloth coverings on the rickety table which served as a pulpit. Someday, perhaps the church could afford to purchase better furniture. Maybe they would also be able to pay their pastors salaries they could live on.

He sighed and sat down to wait for the teenagers. Despite the difficulties, he enjoyed the work. Elijah took out his Swahili Bible and began to go over the passage for his sermon in the market. As he wrote down a few tentative ideas, he wondered how long the Endo would have to wait for God's Word in their own mother tongue. He began to pray for the Bible translation project. He had decided to visit Ken Greenlee, the Wycliffe Bible translator, when he heard shouts of laughter from the young people coming to practice their songs. Perhaps he would visit Ken in the morning.

That night, Elijah lay down and fell asleep as soon as his head touched the pillow. The eerie, almost human cry of the goats in their enclosures was so common place it no longer registered in his conscious thoughts. The sighing of the wind among the acacia and small ebony trees was like a lullaby. Small pieces of grass occasionally filtered down from the roof, dislodged by lizards scurrying above his head in search of insects.

Yet as he slept, an alien sound and smell intruded into his dreams, forcing him to sudden alertness. Fire! Smoke! The roof of his hut was ablaze.

Elijah had no time to grab his clothes. Snatching his Bible and a few books from his bookcase, he fled into the night just as the cedar posts holding up the roof ignited. In a spectacular display of sparks, the entire upper structure of the hut collapsed onto the bed he had recently occupied. A brilliant array lit up the darkness around him, obscuring the stars.

His bike, his clothes, most of his books — all his possessions were gone. He put the few books he'd saved into a small cardboard box in his yard and ran to get relatives to help. As soon as he left the yard, those who had torched his roof picked up the box and tossed it into the flames. Satisfied with the destruction they had wrecked, they slipped away silently into the night. The intruders considered themselves enemies of his family and his Christian beliefs, so they had taken this traditional way of showing their hatred.

The next morning, as Pastor Elijah walked through the ruin of his home, forlorn, he bent down suddenly. On the floor lay his Bible, turned to ash, but still in the form of the book. On the cover he could clearly read, "Holy Bible".

To him this was a message from his Lord. Even in the midst of undeserved destruction, God was present. God would work out his future and would be faithful to him if he remained faithful to his task.

The next afternoon, he went to see Ken Greenlee. Through contacts in America, Ken eventually replaced virtually all of Elijah's library. Many new reference books were among those provided by Christians who heard what had occurred.

Looking Inward: When we are facing a dark moment, we often cannot imagine how God will work things out. Yet, he uses those times to teach us to be completely dependent on Him. Out of the ashes of our lives, He brings hope.

Looking Outward: When others wrong us, it is easy to allow anger and bitterness to well up inside. When a person hurts us unjustly, it can be difficult to forgive. Yet, Jesus challenges us to love our enemies, to be kind to those who persecute us. This is the ultimate challenge to our Christianity.

S. T. O.
Wycliffe Bible Translators

Fifty-one

Alphonse
Counting the Risks

Uganda

But no man can die cheerfully or comfortably who lives not in a constant resignation of the time and season of his death unto the will of God, as well as himself with respect unto death itself. . . . Without this resolution, without this resignation, no man can enjoy the least solid peace in this world. —John Owen from *On the Glory of Christ*

The civil war in northeastern Uganda raged on. Rebels controlled much of the countryside. Battle lines cut off many innocent people behind the lines, forcing them to the brink of starvation.

Relief efforts into that region were difficult. Any food or aid brought in, by whatever agency, gave the rebels the impression that it came indirectly from the government as a means of weakening the rebels' cause. People were afraid to make the treacherous journey into the areas where many were approaching starvation.

When the people, cattle herdsmen by trade, ran out of food, they began killing off their cattle to eat. Now the cattle were all gone as was their remaining food supplies.

Knowing all the risks, a group of young people with Youth With A Mission accepted the challenge to try to take supplies into that area. Their leader, Alphonse Rwiririza, who was from another part of Uganda, was not familiar with that part of the country, but he agreed to undertake the relief mission.

"We know the rebels felt that if we helped the people we would be helping the government," he said. "This put us in a dangerous position, but people were starving."

The team, using an old pickup truck, began carrying food and other relief supplies into the stricken area. They never lacked opportunities to do evangelism. The people were delighted to see them.

"But, why do you come?" some of them asked, realizing the danger they were facing by entering that rebel-held area.

Alphonse's dark eyes sparkled as he repeated the answer, "We come because of what God has done in our hearts. We want to share the wonderful news of Jesus."

After each food distribution, the group would hold a service and preach the gospel to the gathered crowd. Meeting people's needs means attempting to meet all of their needs—physical as well as spiritual, the group of relief workers reasoned.

Every day they faced danger. But never as critical as the time they were driving out to distribute food, and armed rebels stopped their pickup truck.

Rebels aimed their rifles at our pickup," Alphonse said. *This may be my last day on earth,* he thought. Raising his arms, Alphonse cautiously stepped away from the truck. *God has brought me here; of that I am certain,* he thought, praying silently. *Am I to die at the hands of these rebels? What will become of my team members?*

It was a moment many believers over the centuries have faced. Of such a time, the Apostle Paul wrote: "If we live, we live to the Lord; and if we die, we die to the Lord. Therefore, whether we live or die, we are the Lord's" (Romans 14:8). It was not a time to question God; it was a time, despite the terror of the moment, to put faith in God.

Suddenly there came a voice from a clump of brush beyond the road, speaking the local language. "Let our friend go," the voice said.

Recalling that scene later, Alphone spoke softly—reverently. "Whether it was an angel—and this would be hard to believe—or whether it was another rebel, I still do not know," he said. "But the rifles were lowered, and we were waved on our way."

Looking Inward: God is more concerned about our reaction to what happens to us than he is about the things that happen to us. He is able to help us, no matter what the circumstances. Through it all, He wants us to believe in Him.

Looking Outward: The evil one never challenges us when we are taking our ease. It is when we are in the way of danger for the sake of God's kingdom that the evil one becomes active to stop God's work through us.

W.W.
Youth With A Mission (YWAM)

Fifty-two

Too Little
Too Late

India

Compassion does not expend its force simply saying, "Be ye warmed; be ye clothed," but drives us to our knees in prayer for those who need Christ and his grace. —E. M. Bounds from *The Essentials of Prayer*

A large orange sun hung low in the sky. Two men trudged the dusty streets of Calcutta. One of the men was Allen Lim, the Singapore director of Youth With a Mission, the guest of the other man, a leader in the local church in Calcutta.

They found themselves pushed along with the crowd on its way to the nearby banks of the Ganges River. The people felt it was important to get there before dark to bathe in its muddy waters. Nowhere else did these devout Hindus find cleansing for their souls.

Every now and then, as they seemed to carom off other bodies, scurrying along the twisted crowded streets, someone would look strangely at the light-skinned man. They hardly noticed the taller dark-skinned Indian church leader walking beside him.

The men were on a walking tour of the city, trying to decide where the YWAM teams should set up for street witnessing by a team of young people coming from Singapore in the next few days.

As dusk approached, the crowd seemed even thicker. Most of them looked neither right nor left—everyone with single-minded intent was heading for the sacred river to bathe.

The crowd seemed to lurch, bumping into each other, and the people up ahead stepped around something lying in the street at their feet. Once past the obstacle, they looked ahead again, hardly breaking stride.

When the two men came nearer to the object lying in the street, they saw it was a feeble old man, frail, wrapped only in a loin cloth. They could see he was hardly breathing. The crowd seemed to push them forward. Soon the old man was out of their sight, but not quite out of mind.

We could have stopped, Allen thought. *But what could we have done?* Several times during the evening, as they approached the river, the sight of the old man sprawled on the crowded street came back to mind.

In order to get a better view of the city, the two men hired a boat. Darkness was beginning to close in and the crowd began moving back the other way. Soon they found themselves again, pushed along by the crowd. Allen wondered if the old man would still be there.

How much he realized that the scene unfolding around him was almost a parable of many lives. We see human needs, and we feel the urge to do something about them. But the crowd, things, people, other duties, more attractive sights cause us to be swept along until the unpleasant sight of what should be done fades from our minds.

Above the noise of the crowd, Allen sensed a quiet voice calling to his spirit. Soon it became a stronger urge: "Go back."

We could do something, he reasoned. *We could see if the old man was still alive and take him to the shelter that the famous nun, Mother Theresa, had started. There he could at least die with dignity.*

Elbows jabbed their ribs; feet tangled with theirs; the unrelenting mob moved on until they came to the place where the old man lay. Bending down, they touched the old man's arm, now grown cold. They were too late.

Looking Inward: Night comes quickly—all over the world. Jesus said, and we must learn to say, "I must work the works of Him who sent me while it is day; the night is coming when no man can work" (John 9:4). The will to do God's work begins within us as we make the commitment to be all we can be to others.

Looking Outward: There are many along our path today—not physically dying like the old man in Calcutta—who are approaching spiritual death. The world crowds us in the other direction, but God's inner voice says, "Go back."

S.T.O.
Youth With A Mission

266 Osborn, Susan Titus